SEE ME

A Fly By Boys Novel

H L MULLER

H. L. Muller is Australian, and this book is written in United Kingdom/Australian English.

ISBN: 978-0-6488610-3-4

Cover design by: Avdal Designs

Editing: Salt & Sage Books

Lyrics: Lukasz Muller

Sensitivity Read: BlindBeta

Publisher: H. L. Muller

Author Note:

Dedication

For Hayden, Always.

Playlist

These are some songs that Cecilia and Maverick listen too,
and that I enjoyed while writing this book.
Animal – Def Leppard
Daisies – Katy Perry
The Pretender – Foo Fighters
S.O.S. – Jonas Brothers
Malibu – Miley Cyrus
Oh Cecilia! (Breaking My Heart) - The Vamps
Waking Up In Vegas – Katy Perry
Love Drunk – Boys Like Girls
Watermelon Sugar – Harry Styles
Sucker – Jonas Brothers
Little Things – One Direction
Monkey Wrench – Foo Fighters
Somebody to You – The Vamps
She's Kinda Hot – 5 Seconds of Summer
What A Man Gotta Do – Jonas Brothers
Teenage Dream – Katy Perry
Play My Music – Jonas Brothers
Love Bites – Def Leppard

Last First Kiss – One Direction
Golden – Harry Styles
Pour Some Sugar On Me – Def Leppard

Prologue - Maverick

I THOUGHT I had things pretty good in high school. I had my pick of all the girls, and I loved them and left them like I think any straight teen boy would do, given the opportunity.

Ever since our album went platinum, my rock star image combined with my good looks ensures that I am the guy every girl wants to be with. Sometimes it's like they're getting off just from talking to me. Yes, I know that sounds vain—but how vain is it when it's the truth? I was *People*'s "Sexiest Man Alive" last year.

In the beginning, I felt on top of the fucking world—I never had to work for pussy or attention. I was just out sowing my wild oats, as some people would say. I had a new girl every other night—I'm practically the king of one-night stands.

Everywhere we went—on tour, on holidays—it didn't matter. It was like there was a brand on my forehead that read *USE ME FOR A GOOD TIME*. Sure, at first I loved it, but soon it became known to me that these women didn't want *me*—they wanted the hot stud, a carefree night of fun, Mav from Fly By.

I'm no saint, and I'm not saying that I turned them down, but after a while, I started to want something different. What's wrong with me, you may ask? To tell you the truth, I don't know—what I do know, I avoid acknowledging at all costs. As the lead guitarist for Fly By, there's a certain image that I need to maintain. With the public and the record company looking on, I have to be careful with how I'm perceived. I learned early on that I can't give the media leverage. If they know your weaknesses, nothing can prevent them from exploiting you.

I just hope that one day, someone who wants to be with me sees me not as some rock star, but as my real self.

One - Maverick

"THANKS FOR A GREAT TIME TONIGHT," Katie calls over her shoulder as she pushes her way out of my room and—if history has taught me anything—out of my life.

We met a few days ago at an after-party. I thought we hit it off —we chatted all night and exchanged numbers, arranging to meet up tonight. We had drinks and dinner, and she insisted we come back to my place. Well...it's not like I argued the point. I am a horny twenty-two-year-old man, after all.

Alcohol combined with her smoking body and advances, I didn't stand much of a chance and caved. Kisses turned into caresses, which turned into pretty decent sex. Not the best I've ever experienced, but the same was not true for her, if her whimpers of delight were anything to go by.

Two minutes after we were done, she was up and getting dressed. Five minutes later, she was walking out the door without a backwards glance. Not even a "let's do this again" or "when can I see you next."

I had thought she might have actually liked me, might have wanted to actually date me. Wishful thinking on my part.

They never wanted the boy with a bad reputation for anything other than a notch on their bedpost. Clearly, I have bad taste in women. By tomorrow morning, all her girlfriends—who knows, maybe the whole world—will know she slept with The Mav from Fly By.

I get it; it's nothing really to complain about. But fuck, is it so bad for me to at least want her to spend the night? Isn't the woman meant to be the one who tries to turn a one-night stand into a relationship, who hangs around like a bad smell until forcefully removed? That's how my buddies describe their experiences. At this point, I almost wish I had a gold-digging harpy hanging around…almost. I'm not *that* stupid.

I flop back onto my bed, sheets still messy, the smell of sweat and sex lingering in the air. Alone again, and I don't know how to change that.

I wake up and untangle myself from the sheets. It's Sunday and we aren't on tour, so I'm expected home for a family lunch and jam sesh. Happiness bubbles in me at the thought of seeing my family and rocking out with my brothers, who are also my bandmates. Jamming out in the garage at home is different than all the studios and stages. It's just us rocking it, playing whatever we feel like and not for work. I've never regretted our music career, but it is nice to enjoy the music and forget about our fame and the expectations our label Reckless Tunez puts on us.

I have a great, typical, run-of-the-mill family. Mum and Dad were high school sweethearts; they stayed together all through university and beyond. Each other's first everything. They got married right out of uni, Dad joined his family's law firm, and Mum started teaching at the local primary school. A few years later, I joined them, then my brothers came along. The twins, Joel and Charlie, arrived when I was two, followed eighteen months later by Tom, and then baby Ethan a year later.

You might have noticed that Mum is a huge—and I mean *huge* —Tom Cruise fan. We're all named after him and his characters. I clearly got the best name: Maverick. *Top Gun* has to be the best movie Tom Cruise was in, and I'm not ashamed to say I'm proud to be named after it. That's also how we got the name for our band, Fly By.

I feel the need, the need for speed! Has turned into a war chant of sorts, that we say before we go out onstage to perform.

I live in the Gold Coast, a two-hour drive from our hometown, Orlo. I moved to the city shortly after hitting nineteen and now attend uni classes incognito when we aren't touring. Joel, Charlie, and Tom live in apartments near me, but Ethan is still at home, as he's only seventeen. When we won *What it Takes!* three years ago, we were on tour for almost two years, hitting countries and stages I had only dreamed of. It was a bit hard with Ethan only being fourteen when we went on tour, but Reckless Tunez came through with a great tutor for the boys in school, and I attended uni online. For two years, we juggled education and performing—but after so long on the road, we decided to hit pause for a while, giving us downtime for finishing school and writing the next album.

Settled back in Australia, I wanted some time to really party like a rock star. Well, minus all the drugs.

Part of the reason I didn't live in my hometown is it would cramp my style—as Mum says—and mostly, I didn't want to disappoint my parents. Not to say that they would slut-shame me for sleeping around, but I just didn't want them to think of me like that. They're *those* parents. You know, the ones who love and support you endlessly and with whom you genuinely love and have a good relationship. The parents who attend every sporting event or extracurricular activity. They paid for our music lessons, drove us to our first concerts, took us to our audition for *What It Takes!*, the TV competition we won three years ago that launched our careers.

Making the drive out to Orlo this morning is dull and boring. No traffic, nothing to look at. I spend my time playing around with lyrics in my head and using voice-to-text to record them in my phone for later inspection. In our band, we've all had a hand in our music. Some songs are written together, alone or constructed together. We have a deadline for a new album demo in a few weeks, and it still needs one more track.

Pulling into the driveway of my childhood home, I turn off the engine of my car and stare at the house. This house has been the centre of my life's entire orbit. The tree house where I had my first kiss, the driveway where I learned how to ride a bike and dribble a basketball, the garage where I learned how to play guitar and developed a close relationship with my brothers.

No matter how rich I am, how famous I get, or where I go, this will always be my home.

I drag myself out of the car and can already hear my brothers goofing around in the house.

"Joel, leave Ethan alone!" my mother scolds.

"Aw, does the baby need Mummy's protection? Can't stand up for yourself?" Joel coos.

"Oi, I can look after myself, mate. Not my fault you decided to be a dickhead in front of Mum and got caught!"

"HEY!" Dad yells as I open the door, causing everyone to turn and watch me enter.

I was the last to arrive, meaning Joel, Charlie, and Tom probably came up last night. We're all homebodies on some level and enjoy being here with our family.

"MAV-MAN!" they call out at once, rushing me.

They plough into me and I relish in the jumble of hugs, backslaps, and a kiss on the cheek from my mum. As they give me room to breathe, I look around to see what Joel and Ethan were arguing over. There's a video game behind them on pause. I break out laughing.

"What?" Joel asks defensively.

"You two are arguing over that? I could hear you from the street!"

"Not like you're more mature," Charlie interjects, coming to his twin's defence.

"Hey, this is about them, not me!" I protest.

"Char isn't wrong, though," Tom comments.

"It's my turn!" Ethan complains, bringing the attention back to Ethan and Joel's fight. Yep. World-famous musicians reduced to squabbling over a video game.

"No, you just died, it's my turn!" Joel replies.

"If you two morons don't shut it, it will be no one's turn, and I will lock the garage!" Dad yells, and our jaws all drop.

Dad hasn't had to break out the *I'll lock the garage* threat in about five years. He isn't joking, either. Once, he locked us out for a whole week of the school holidays. To this day, none of us have keys to the garage, even though it's our sacred place.

"It's the only way we can ensure you'll actually come into the house to see us!" my mother said when I asked for a set of keys a few years ago.

I can't exactly say she was wrong. As much as we all love our parents, the garage—and our music—is our world. We wouldn't be able to exist without it.

Thankfully, the boys heed his warning and settle down, allowing Joel to take a turn. Today would have been shit if we hadn't been allowed to rock out.

I follow Mum and Dad into the kitchen, where they return to preparing lunch. I give them both another hug and kiss on the cheek before picking up a knife and helping Mum prepare the salad.

"What have you been doing this morning, aside from refereeing the kids' fights?" I ask, genuinely interested in their response. My family has always been really close, and my parents are easily some of the best friends I've ever had. They really nailed the parent/friend divide and always knew what you needed when you needed it.

"We had a great morning, Maverick," Mum replies.

"We went down to the farmers market, and your mum picked up a new planter and decorations for the garden," Dad interjects.

They've always been like that, like a mix and match of individual sentences that blend together.

Mum loves gardening, and with spring just around the corner, I am sure we can expect a lot more purchases in the next few weeks.

"You'll have to show me what you have planned for spring," I say to Mum, "and let me do any heavy lifting."

"Oh please," Mum exclaims, directing a humoured glare at me, "no such thing. That's what that landscaping company you pay for is there to do."

I shrug sheepishly. They've never accepted our money. Anytime we tried to give them money, they say, "You boys worked hard for that money; it isn't ours to take." But I'd figured out if I pay for something directly, they won't reject it.

We had never been poor or struggling, even with five teenage boys in the house at once, but from seeing movies about parents exploiting their famous kids, I kind of expected them to want at least some of our millions. They were adamant they had no claim to our money, though. We compromised: they won't accept direct cash, but they can't stop us from buying things for them.

"Well, I can still help out if you need me, Mum," I offer.

"I know, sweetie." She pats me on the back and starts putting all the food on the dining table. "Can you get your brothers for lunch?"

"LUNCH IS READY," I yell out.

"I could have done that," Mum complains, whacking me in the stomach.

"Yeah, but it worked." I laugh as the boys rush in from the lounge room and we all take our usual seats.

We are all quiet as Mum serves herself first before the rest of us take our turn filling our plates with delicious home-cooked food. Sunday lunches are a mini feast. Today we have BBQ steak and sausages, quiche, garden salad, bread rolls and a baked vegetable dish. A bit of a hotchpotch, but it's all of our favourites.

"So, boys," Dad begins, "how has your week been?"

We go around the table, talking about school, friends, songs, tour information, and the like. I don't mention last night with Katie. It's nothing they haven't heard of before, but I'm just not in the mood to deal with any pity.

Before long, my brothers and I are all in the garage, set up and ready to roll. We've never had a single leader—we're more of a democracy than a dictatorship. We each give input and take each other into consideration.

"What are we starting with today?" Joel asks.

"Who's feeling 'Runaway?'" Ethan asks.

The lyrics for "Runaway" were written by Joel for our new album. We all nod and start playing the song. Muscle memory takes over and my fingers play the song perfectly, plucking over the strings of my guitar, as Joel begins the first verse.

"Brown heels, curly hair, eyes so blue you'd think they're the ocean.

I found you in a cafe downtown, my heartbeat stopped, and the world lost its sound.

Fell in love at first sight, don't know who you are but that's alright.

Are you even a fan of people like me? Long hair, dark clothes and all inked from my head to my feet..."

JOEL HASN'T TOLD us the story behind "Runaway" yet, but I can tell he's still hung up on that woman. It doesn't matter, he'll tell us when he's ready. Nothing—and I mean nothing—

compares to the feeling of playing my guitar with my brothers, rocking out to a song. Whether it's in the garage or in a stadium, it's always the same amazing feeling.

This is exactly what I need after a shitty start to the weekend. We spend the afternoon playing our songs and a few of our favourite covers and playing around with some new material.

Two - Cecilia

"I JUST DON'T KNOW how we can afford it, Cece," my sister Taylor says to me.

"That's okay, Taylor, I understand." We were talking about the Fly By national tour starting February next year. Since they were on *What It Takes!* a few years ago, I've gone to every concert in Queensland. I fell in love with their voices and music the first time I heard them. They have this unique take on rock that mesmerises me.

According to Taylor, they're incredibly attractive young men who make the female population go crazy, and tickets sell out on the first day. Some talk show hosts have even claimed the only reason they are so popular is because they are hot. For me, I don't care what they look like, I find voices, attitude, and knowledge attractive. Their voices, and their music, are amazing. Their songs are so descriptive and emotive, I feel like I can see the scenes they depict.

Being blind impacts my life a lot, but music is something that I can enjoy just as much as the next person. Music is the core of my life. I can find any song to suit a mood, a feeling, a moment, or a memory. I was born blind and have never been able to look at art, I watch movies with audio descriptions and I'm sure I interpret colours different to a sighted person.

"I feel bad, Cece," Taylor continues. "I know how much it means to you to go. Maybe we can check again closer to the date and see if anyone wants to resell their tickets cheap."

We have a limited income; Taylor is a manager at the local library, but I rely solely on my Disability Support Payment, and our parents aren't much better off. They have always been there to support us, but lately Mum lost her job and they only have Dad's income now while she looks for new employment. The tickets for their tour are dropping the same week our quarterly bills are due, and we don't have any spare cash.

"Okay, Tay," I reply, knowing that we likely won't be able to afford tickets later either. "What do you have on your agenda for today?"

"I have work until 7 p.m. Do you think you'll be okay to get the bus home from uni? And you can order in for dinner tonight."

"Yes, I can get the bus no issues." I sigh. I have been blind for twenty years and know how to look after myself while out in public, yet sometimes my family still treats me like I'm incompetent. I click the button on my watch to announce the time.

"NINE SEVENTEEN," a robotic voice calls out.

"I have to get to the campus, Taylor," I say while getting up and going into my bedroom. My wardrobe is organised into shirts, skirts, pants, and dresses. Sorted between draws and hanging spaces. When out and about shopping I have a colour scanner and have learnt the different textures of materials. Rifling through the draws, I pull out a printed t-shirt and a pair of jeans, dressing quickly with my Dr. Marten boots. I brush my fingers through my hair, picking up my laptop bag and handbag, making sure to secure my voice recorder in my pocket. Heading back out to the kitchen, I embrace my sister and say farewell for the day.

"Do I look okay?" When I was younger Taylor used to pressure me to change my clothes, urging me to conform and fit in. It took a strain on my confidence and one day I couldn't take it any longer. I snapped. I yelled and protested, saying many things that I regret to this day. Fortunately, once we sat down with Mum and talked it over, I realised Taylor thought she was helping, and I confessed how I her controlling and treating me like an invalid made me feel. Since then, I have experimented and done more research into what styles, colours, and fabrics I like. And occasionally, like today, I ask her about my outfit, to make sure it doesn't clash or isn't too eccentric.

"Beautiful as always," she replies, helpfully handing me my sunglasses and cane. I exit the apartment and make my way to university.

The bus driver knows me. He always ensures I safely dismount the bus at the correct stop and tells me the right direction to the campus if he has to stop in a different spot.

Today I have two classes: Music History and Finance. I hope one day I will be able to find work in the industry, preferably as a producer, finalising albums with artists to make sure they are perfect. It would be a dream come true to work with Fly By, but I know my chances of meeting them—let alone working with them—would be extremely slim. Besides, they are established with a record label and already have producers. There is no way that I would be able to convince them to work with someone like me, compared to what they already have.

I make my way to Music History and sit down in my usual seat at the front of the class. I like to arrive at least five minutes early, allowing time for me to have my laptop and voice recorder set up for the lecture. Typing and voice to text has been a game changer in my education and livelihood. I am able to write out my notes for all my classes and the professors are helpful, providing me electronic copies of any worksheets.

This university has been a godsend to me. Not only are they accepting of everyone—disability, identity, and sexuality—but they allow me to do any exams verbally with a scribe, or with voice to text and typing. I have audiobooks of all required textbooks and when I ask, my professors often record explanations just for me, or descriptions of what they write on the board during lectures.

I do not like the term "teacher's pet," but I'm pretty sure that is what I am. I answer any question that I can in my lectures and actually enjoy coming to classes, unlike some of the other people I have met. The number of times someone arrives late to class or falls asleep mid-lecture drives me insane. If you don't want to be here, why enrol? Uni isn't compulsory like high school is, and there are so many jobs out there that you don't need a degree for. If you are studying for a career that you will love, you wouldn't treat the classes like some of the students here do.

I understand that university years are where most people go crazy, going on benders, doing drugs, sleeping around, or letting their freak-flag fly—and power to them. I don't mean to tell them what they can and can't do with their time. But it would be nice if they were considerate of the people around them and the impact that they have on our lives.

"Pop rock dates back to the early 1950s, where singers such as Elvis Presley and Chuck Berry performed, accompanied with the guitar and bass guitar," Professor Jonson began. "This music was controversial but was catchy and popular amongst the public. It still held original hints of rock, which has changed over the years to what we know today."

Music History has to be one of my favourite classes, and for our current assignment we are focusing on the development of rock music, one of my favourite genres. Professor Jonson highlights some of the most popular bands and artists over the last seventy years, and ends the lecture playing a mashup of pop-rock songs—ending with Fly By's most popular song, "Seen."

It was the first song I heard from them, and I'd instantly loved it.

"This song is an example of the range that rock music has. This song—although acoustic with no electric guitars—still falls under the rock banner," Professor Jonson says over the lyrics.

I seriously had to restrain myself from singing along and dancing around to the music, allowing myself only to tap my fingers and feet in time with the beat.

Packing up from another awesome lesson, I dread my class after lunch. All of my music classes are my favourite and ending the day with Finance is a bit of a killjoy. Finance is a class I struggle with, as I cannot see the equations that are so necessary to understand the content. Unfortunately, the course is required for my business degree.

I grab my cane and start making my way back through the campus to the cafeteria to meet up with some friends for lunch.

Three - Maverick

I DUCK MY HEAD, drawing my hoodie up to cover my face. I haven't seen any paparazzi yet, but sometimes they follow me and I don't realize. I usually don't mind them—it's a part of the fame, and the fans who made us famous make our jobs possible. But today I just don't have the time or patience to deal with them, and I don't want them to see me near campus. Everyone has mobile phones, too, and it just takes one of them to rat me out. It is speculated that I attend school here, but to have it confirmed would have the campus swarming with fans and paps. I don't want to impact everyone else's study with that.

I am running late for my last lecture of the day. I left campus for lunch and am now paying for it. I hightail across the court-yard, keeping my head down, focusing too much on concealing myself than what is going on around me, and I knock into another body. We both tumble to the ground, a tangle of limbs and books.

"Oh my god, I am so sorry!" I exclaim as I start to detangle our legs.

"Ah!" a delicate feminine voice calls out.

I pull myself free and realise it is a girl I crashed into. Well, a woman. She looks to be in her early twenties, with fiery red hair that is messed about and knotted from our collision. Her face is covered in huge dark sunglasses, preventing me from seeing anything other than her plump pink lips.

"Are you okay?" I ask while collecting my books and her bag.

"You should watch where you are going, imbecile!" she scolds. Her voice is musical—peaceful and soothing, not suiting the harsh frown on her lips.

"I know, I am sorry. I was…" I trail off, not sure why she was still sitting on the ground and why she wasn't going nuts after seeing my face. I know not everyone is a fan of Fly By, but with our media coverage, everyone knows who we are. It was strange to not cause a reaction.

"Are you okay? Are you injured?" I ask, concerned.

"I'm just dandy," she replies, voice dripping with sarcasm. "I thought I would just familiarise myself with the ground because an insensitive asshole knocked me over, and I don't know where I am now!"

"Huh?" I ask, confused.

"Well!" she exclaims. She stands up, looking disoriented. "Are you still there?"

"Um, yes?" I ask, standing right in front of her. What kind of question is that?

My eyes rake over her body—she is about a foot shorter than me, curves everywhere a man could want them. I stare at her tits longer than I should, surprised to find my brothers faces staring back at me. It's a Fly By shirt from our first concert in Brisbane.

"You like Fly By?" I ask. It's strange that she still hasn't recognised me. Maybe I can make up for this accident with a CD or tickets or something.

"I have to get to class, asshole," she replies, ignoring my question. "Since you crashed into me, the least you can do is help me in the right direction."

"Do you need a map?"

"What part of this isn't adding up for you? Sunglasses, cane… cane! Where the fuck is my cane?" Panic edging her voice.

"Your cane?" I ask, still confused about what is happening. I spot the white cane, rolled slightly away from our encounter. The moment my eyes land on it, I realise what my stupid brain hasn't picked up yet. Fuck. I knocked over a blind person. She must think I am the most self-absorbed prick ever —hell, she wouldn't even be wrong half the time.

"Uh—" I stammer. "Just wait here a sec…" I walk over to collect the cane and ensure that it is still in one piece. "Here you go," I say, placing it in her outstretched hand. She runs her hands over it, feeling for the bottom and placing it on the ground.

"Now, can you tell me where I need to go?" she asks, clearly indignant and over her encounter with me.

"Yes, of course. Where are you heading?"

"Building C, Room 4."

"I'm in that class too—I'll walk with you there. How can I help?"

She extends her hand out to me. Not knowing what she wants, I place my hand in hers.

"Ugh, idiot." She drops my hand and extends hers again. "I want my bag."

Of course. That's the obvious reason she extended her hand, not to hold mine. I really am an idiot. I place the straps of her bag on her extended palm.

"You—uh—might want to fix your hair," I try to say as kindly as possible.

"Mmph." She brushes her fingers through her luscious red locks, giving herself a beautiful windswept look. "How's that?"

"M-much better," I stammer out. What is it about this woman that is causing me to stutter like a kindergartener? "I'm sorry. I really can't say that enough."

"Ugh, it's fine, whatever. Can we get to class now, please? I hate being late."

"Okay." I take the hand she has offered out to me and guide her towards our finance class. After a few steps in the right direction, I drop her hand and walk next to her.

"Thanks…what is your name?"

"Maverick."

"Cecilia."

"A gorgeous name for a gorgeous woman."

"Please don't. I'm not in the mood for flirty boys today."

"Okay." I fall silent, keeping pace with her as we walk through the courtyard together. "So, Cecilia, tell me about you," I say after a while.

"I'm blind, I got walked into and knocked over by a random man I have never met before, and I am late for class. What about you, Maverick?" she replies sassily.

I laugh, causing my shoulders to bump into Cecilia. Her breath catches and she missteps, tripping over her feet. Reaching out, I catch her before she can hug the pavement for the second time today, my laughter abruptly cut off.

"Are you okay?" I ask, genuinely concerned. "Did I trip you again?" Did my shoulder hitting hers cause her to trip? Or, in our crash earlier, did she hit her head? Could she have a concussion?

"I'm fine!" she exclaims, a slight blush creeping out from underneath her huge sunglasses.

"Okay, okay," I say, releasing her. "How long have you been in this class?" I ask, letting the topic fall.

"Why do you care?"

"Just making conversation. We can walk in silence if you prefer."

She harrumphs. I have never heard of a *harrumph* being attractive, yet it is something Cecilia has mastered.

"I have been at this university for two years and a half, and I have been in the finance class—that I am now late for—since the start of the semester... like everyone else. So that's, like, eight weeks now."

"Mmm."

"Mmm? What kind of response is 'mmm?'"

"The kind where I am wondering how I have been in the same room as you for eight weeks and haven't noticed you."

"Well, you must be pretty self-absorbed to not notice the plain blind girl at the front of the classroom—"

I snort, cutting her off. "You are *not* plain." With fiery red hair and that sparkly personality that I am only just beginning to see, I can tell she is not plain.

She remains silent and ignores me as we continue walking.

"Wait!" She stops in her tracks, a delicate scowl twisting her lips into a frown.

"What? What's wrong?" I ask, panic edging my voice.

"We passed the classroom!"

"H-how do you know that?"

"We are at the bottom of a staircase, there isn't a staircase on the way to the classroom."

"UH," I reply sheepishly, "I may have walked past the class-room 'cause I was enjoying walking with you and didn't notice." I cautiously turn her around and walk us back in the direction of our Finance class. Unfortunately, she goes silent again. How stupid of me to not think about how vulnerable Cecilia must be feeling right now. She's relying on a strange man to tell her where she is.

"Sorry we are late, Professor," I call out as we enter the room. "I ran into Cecilia and held her up."

"Okay, Mav, please take a seat and we can continue," Professor Jones replies. He is one of the professors who will let me get away with anything. I see heads turn to look at us—namely, me. I lead Cecilia over to a pair of empty chairs and sit down next to her, glad to realise people aren't paying us too much attention anymore. I can tell she is trying to ignore my presence as she pulls off her sunglasses, showing me the most beautiful face and eyes I have ever seen. Her nose has a spat-tering of freckles, and her eyes are a beautiful shade of green.

I sit there like a fool, mesmerised by her beauty. I barely notice as she pulls out a voice recorder and MacBook. Until I see a huge crack across the screen. *FUCK.*

I lean over in my seat. "I'm sorry, C. The screen of your Mac is broken," I whisper, trying to not disturb the professor again.

"No!" she whispers back to me. "No, no, no, no, no."

I watch her panic, and a feeling of dread swamps me. This must be her lifeline. It must have all her uni work and be set up with all her preferences to help her with...well, everything.

"It must have happened when I knocked you over. I'll pay to fix it—"

"Damn right you will," she replies, cutting me off, relief filling her voice.

"I can take you after class," I offer before my mind even has time to process it. "I can drive you to wherever you need to go and get the screen fixed then. Is that okay?"

She nods and falls silent, focusing on the rest of the lecture. Cecilia asks questions here and there to clarify points that Jones is making. I type out all the notes for the lecture, ensuring I get everything down. I am not normally this thorough, but if Cecilia isn't able to write her own notes today, I have to make sure I get as much info as possible for her. As the lecture draws to an end, I signal Jones over.

"I need you to hold everyone back so we can exit," I murmur to him.

His eyes flick over to Cecilia. "Okay, Cecilia and Mav, you two can go."

She and I quickly pack up. She walks out of the room as I trail behind her.

Cecilia stops just outside the classroom. Standing next to her, I offer her my arm. "Do you want to take my arm so I can lead you to my car?" I ask.

"Okay." She reaches out and grips onto my elbow, her small hand stretching to reach around my arm.

I draw up my hoodie again, keeping my face shadowed as I guide us through to the student car park, paying more attention to my surroundings this time. As we approach my car, I announce to her how far away the car is, and when we get to it, I make sure that she found a spot to put her bag and found her seatbelt. I stare at her for a moment, feeling like a bit of a stalker before shaking myself out of it and getting us on the road.

Before we exit the car park, she has her phone out and is making a phone call.

Four - Cecilia

"HEY CECE, HOW ARE YOU DOING?" Taylor's voice comes through the phone.

"Hey Tay, I am good. Are you busy?" She's at work by now, and the last thing I want to do is disrupt her day.

"Hold on a sec, I'll just head into the office so I don't disturb the patrons." I hear her moving around and a door closing before her voice is in my ear again. "Okay, what's up? You don't normally call at this time of the day. Is everything okay?" Panic edges her voice.

"I'm fine. An idiot on campus today crashed into me and broke my laptop screen." I run my free hand nervously over the luxurious seat underneath me, the soft leather buttery under my fingertips.

"We don't have the kind of money to fix that, Cece," she replies, her voice tense.

"I know. Maverick is driving me to the store now so he can pay to have it fixed."

"Maverick? Who's Maverick? You've never mentioned him before."

"Well, I only met him today when he bulldozed me, now, didn't I?"

I hear a soft chuckle from Maverick as he drives.

"I'm not sure if I am okay with a random man driving you around—are you sure it's safe?"

"That's why I am calling you to let you know where I am going. If I don't tell you I got home safe in a few hours, then call the cops."

"Hey," Maverick says, loud enough for my sister to hear him through the phone, "I am not crazy or a creep. I will ensure C gets home safe. My fault she is in this position, only fair that I fix it."

"Saying you aren't a creep is exactly what a creep would do," I reply to him, a smile tingling at the corner of my mouth.

"Well, fuck." Maverick's deep rumbling laugh fills the car. "What can I say to set you ladies at ease?"

"He's flirting with you, C," Taylor whispers through the phone.

"I know, he has been doing it all afternoon," I reply. I realise his nickname for me is certainly flirty.

"You're flirting back!" she exclaims.

"N-no, I'm not," I reply.

"OMG," she squeals. "You soooo are! Okay, okay, I gotta get back to work. Have fun, sis! Let me know when you get home, and I can't wait to hear all about your mystery man!"

"No," I groan, but the call is already dead. Taylor is a romantic down to her last cell, and nothing I do now will sway her belief that I am destined to be with Maverick.

"What's wrong?" Maverick asks. I'm sure today will go down in history as the one where he has asked "what's wrong" and "are you okay" the most times.

"Nothing," I mutter, slipping my phone back into my jeans pocket.

He remains quiet, accepting my dismissal of the conversation, and the song on the radio fills the car. It's a cruel trick of fate that "Oh Cecilia" by The Vamps is playing. I love-hate this song. It's fun and pop-y, which I love, but since it has my name, it's like I'm the butt of a joke. The number of times I have heard my sister singsong my name in tune with the music is immeasurable. It was really cute the first few times, but after a hundred odd times, it is just plain annoying.

"Cecilia, you're breaking my heart, you're shaking my confidence daily—" Maverick laughs, singing along. I repress a shiver at the way my name sounds rolling off his tongue. The song does not do his voice justice. It's deep and husky. Maverick would be better off singing '80s love ballads.

"Are you a fan of The Vamps?" I ask him, speaking over the music. As much as I want Maverick to continue singing, I don't want to listen to this song.

"Not necessarily, but I am a fan of all music."

Something we have in common, then—not that I would admit that when he is being flirty like this.

"Really?" I ask, barely containing my curiosity. Music is a subject that I can talk about endlessly.

"Yes," he replies, somehow conveying both enthusiasm and hesitancy. "I mainly listen to rock bands, but I have a few other country and pop artists that I frequently listen to. What about you?"

"I listen to anything," I answer honestly. "I have favourites, of course, but overall, I can listen to any genre, decade, or version of music. Music is the core of my life. It helps me exist. I am able to experience it just as well as a sighted person with no missed visuals. It is something that doesn't need to be added too or described. Even though they are more common nowadays, audio descriptions are not always available. Some TV shows, movies, even live theatre, don't have that available. Often Taylor, or my parents will do this for me when they are around—but with music I can be independent. I can experience concerts and dance…" I trail off sheepishly. "Uh sorry. Music is kind of a passion subject for me. I tend to rant about it."

"I love music, too, so I can understand why it gets to you. Who's your favourite?"

"Fly By."

He coughs and splutters.

"Are you okay?" I ask, concerned.

"Yeah, C, I am fine," Maverick replies in a squeak, clearing his throat before he continues. "So, Fly By, huh? What do you like about them?"

"How hot they look," I sigh, pitching my voice to sound like their teen groupies.

"Wait…what?" Maverick replies with confusion, and I laugh.

Unfortunately, it's the kind of laughter that gets away from you until you are wheezing and on the verge of peeing your pants. I gasp for breath, managing to get myself under control.

"I'd say I'm sorry, but I'm really not. It was a joke. I, uh, like to make jokes about my lack of vision. It's dark humour, but I think it's funny." And it makes people more comfortable around me. "To answer your question, I like their sound. They also are really influential in the music industry, they have done several shows to raise money for charities, and I heard about them completing a "Make a Wish" last year for an ill child. I like that they are invested in the world around them and are not self-absorbed."

He is silent for a moment before replying, "Yeah, okay, that makes sense. What about your favourite song, then?"

"'Seen.'"

"Really? What draws you to it? Or is it just because it's a popular song?"

"It is their best-selling song, but that's not why I love it. I love the raw emotion in the lyrics. I know that desire to be seen by more than you appear. People look at me and see the blind girl. They don't see my love for my family and eating caramel ice cream. Don't see the Cecilia who likes to go to the beach and loves rollercoasters. The words just speak to me. Mind you, 'Inverted' is my second-favourite."

"You know that song is just about sex, right?"

"Come on! Who doesn't? With lyrics like **'I've never seen a woman move the way that you do. With your body so sweet that I'd never forget the taste too. The things you do to my head, when you're in my bed.'** Fly By comes across as this wholesome teen/young adult-centric band, but that song just drips sex appeal."

"Hmmm."

"What about you? Do you listen to them?"

"Haha, a little bit. Yeah, I guess you could say that."

"Why do you like them?"

"Umm—they're genuine. The bond they have together as brothers is magical. They have an interesting history and story about how they hit it big."

"Yeah, I found them on *What It Takes!*"

"Ah, so you've been a Flyer since the beginning, aye?"

Flyer was the name given to their fan group when they were on the TV show. I am kind of surprised he knows the term.

"Yeah, I love them. I've been to every concert that I can. Even though I can't see it, the majority of my shirts are band merch —and bedroom décor."

"Wow. You really are a big fan. Have you ever met them?"

"Oh, I wish. We always have to get the furthest seats, as that's all we can afford. One day I hope I can meet them. What about you?"

"Ah, yeah, I've met them."

"No. Freaking. Way. Are they just as amazing in person?"

"Haha yeah, they are all great. Who's your favourite?"

"Probably Joel. He strikes me as the most emotional."

Five - Maverick

JOEL. *Joel!* This amazing, beautiful woman's favourite is Joel? Her favourite song is *my* song.

"Wait," she interjects before I can even get my head around what she just said. "You have the same name as the guitarist, don't you?"

"Uh—yeah, I do."

"Most people only know him as 'the Mav.' The total bad boy and the eldest of the brothers."

"Mmhmm." I don't know how to respond to this. I really should tell her who I am. But telling her now will just ruin everything, and soon she will be out of my life, anyway.

Cecilia is the first person to treat me like a normal human being—outside of my family—in god knows how long. Knowing she is a fan will just turn this into Stalker Central. I am better off fixing her computer and never talking to her again—except I don't *want* to never talk to her again. I want to know her better than she knows herself. I want her to be the one who could finally see past the "bad boy persona," behind "the Mav" and just see me.

As I park my car at the mall, I realise just how crazy my thoughts are.

The only good thing about pretending to be normal in public is if you act naturally enough and have the right disguise, fans never really believe it's you. You are just this guy who happens to look a lot like someone who might be famous, especially if you are somewhere they won't expect you to be. Like at a shopping centre.

"I am going to get out of the car and come over to help you. Is that okay?" I ask Cecilia.

I watch her throat bob as she swallows, then nods.

Exiting the car, I quickly remove my hoodie, showcasing my hot pink T-shirt with a random abstract print and pull on a baseball cap and a pair of sunglasses. Not exactly "incognito" as you would expect, but no one would think I was the *actual* Mav of Fly By dressed like this. Hiding in plain sight and all that.

Moving around the car, I open the passenger door and announce to Cecilia where my arm is for her to grasp and ease her out of the car.

"Where are we?" she asks once she is firmly on her feet.

"At the mall, so we can go to the Apple Store here. Are—are you comfortable holding onto my arm so I can guide you?" I ask hesitantly. I don't want to be rude and over-help her or act like she's incompetent, because I know she isn't. But I still don't know if what I am doing is acceptable or offensive. I have never spent any time around a blind person before.

"Yes, thank you."

I offer her my arm and start walking us towards the entrance closest to the Apple Store.

Her fingers brush lightly against the hair on my forearm, as if she is caressing me—but that can't be right.

"You took off your shirt?" she puzzles, causing me to laugh.

"No, just my hoodie," I explain. "I'm not shirtless. It was just a bit much with the extra layers." I keep reasoning like an idiot. Why am I babbling about layers?

"Okay…?" she trails off like it's a question. Man, could I be any more awkward?

We remain silent as I guide her through the car park, only talking as I explain avoiding any holes and pointing out the steps. We enter the mall, and as I'd hoped, no one identifies me. C removes her glasses now that we are inside. I noticed she did that in the classroom too. I wonder why that is. I leave my sunglasses on to conceal my face and lead Cecilia towards the Apple Store—which is thankfully empty, except for a handful of employees.

"Hi, welcome to Apple. How may we assist you today?" a young man asks us from the entrance.

"We need to get my computer fixed. The screen is broken, but I can't lose all my settings or documents," Cecilia says. I stand quietly next to her, hoping that these workers don't identify me and tip off C.

"Of course. Follow me," he replies. Cecilia is still holding onto my elbow, and I lead her over to the booth, where he indicates for us to sit. "Please wait here and I'll get a team member over to assist you."

Cecilia gets herself situated as he leaves, and I sit next to her. She carefully removes her laptop from her bag and places it on the table in front of us.

"Hi, I am Georgi," a perky blonde says, sitting down with us, "I hear you need a new screen for your MacBook. Can I have a look at it?"

"Yes, of course," Cecilia answers.

"Ooh! You like Fly By?" Georgi asks while opening the laptop.

"Um, yeah," C replies sheepishly, and I peek over at the MacBook to see that it is covered with stickers of Fly By concerts and album names, and some lyrics too. Clearly, Cecilia really is a superfan.

As Georgi went over the computer, I found myself daydreaming about telling Cecilia who I am. Would she faint? That's probably not a good thing. Would she hate me for keeping it a secret? I didn't lie about my name, at least. That has to count for something. Would she turn into a stalker or never speak to me again?

"So, I have good news and bad news," Georgi says, startling me from my thoughts. "The bad news is we no longer make this version of MacBook and don't have the replacements screens to be able to repair it—"

"What!" Cecilia exclaims, "No! Not now! That computer has lasted me like ten years. I—I can't live without it." Her voice breaks on a sob.

Without hesitation, I wrap my arm around her shoulder in comfort. "It's okay, C, we will sort something out. You said there was good news?" I ask Georgi.

"Yes! If you buy a new one today, I can transfer all your software, documents, and preferences to the new MacBook."

"I can't afford a new one," she moans, hanging her head.

"Hey, I'm paying, remember?" I murmur to her before turning to Georgi. "Do you have the latest top-of-the-range MacBook available for C to look at, to determine it's the one she wants?" I cringe inwardly. Is it cruel to say things like "look" and "see?" There is a whole world here that I have never stepped foot in, and now I constantly feel like a bumbling ignorant fool.

"Of course," Georgi replies, walking off as Cecilia says, "I can't let you do that, Maverick. It's too much. I can't accept it."

"Yeah, you can accept it. Trust me, I can afford it. And getting a new model will give you the latest technology to assist you. Please let me help you by buying this. It would mean a lot to me to make it up to you—replacing what I broke."

Cecilia groans as Georgi returns with the display MacBook.

"Here you go. Have a play around and make sure it's what you want."

"Has the keyboard changed since my version?" Cecilia asks while reaching out to the MacBook.

"No, the basic layout, commands, and keys have remained the same."

Cecilia turns on VoiceOver and I watch as she starts to navigate her way through the computer, Georgi pointing out new features as they go. It's strange to realise how much I take for granted as a sighted person.

C turns to me, a huge smile stretching across her face, lighting up her green eyes. Making eye contact with her, I feel like something just hit me in my chest as my breath hitches. "Are you sure?" she asks breathlessly.

Unable to talk, I nod before remembering that she cannot see me. "Yeah. Yup. Yes," I blabber. "Um, I mean—yes, I am sure." I turn to Georgi. "Can you please get the new one set up and all the information transferred over as you said? Where should I pay?"

"Of course, I will start on that now," Georgi replies. "When you are ready, please join me at the register to pay."

"Did you want to wait here?" I ask Cecilia as Georgi walks off.

"W-what?" she stammers, like I said something shocking.

Six - Cecilia

"DO you want to stay here while I pay and Georgi sets up the computer, or do you want to walk over with me?" Maverick asks.

He asks me—actually asks me. It shouldn't be a big deal, but to me, it is. I sit here, mouth opening and closing like a fish, just marvelling at the unique creature that is this man.

"I'm sorry?" I ask, coming back to the conversation.

"Why are you sorry?" he asks, concern edging his voice.

"I don't understand." I start rambling. (One thing to know about me—I ramble when I am nervous.) "No one outside of my family has really ever asked me what I *want* to do. I am always treated like this invalid just because I cannot see. I've only known you for a few hours, and you have treated me completely different to how everyone else does. You have been kind and courteous asking me for my opinion, what I want, and what I am comfortable with. I—I have never had someone do that before…" I trail off, getting a grip of myself.

Longing to see his face rushes through me. I accepted my condition long ago, yet this is one of the few times I wish I could see. I wonder what he looks like. Do his eyebrows furrow when he thinks? Is his smile uneven?

Outside of my family, I have always been made to feel like something was wrong with me—except now, with Maverick.

"Why are you sorry about that?" he exclaims. "Everyone else should be sorry that they treat you that way! You are a normal person. Why would I treat you any differently?"

"I'm just not used to it, as sad as it is. You must be one of a kind, Maverick."

He scoffs. "I am not special because I treat you like a human being."

"You shouldn't be, but you are nonetheless. Anyway, I will wait here while you pay and she finishes up transferring my data."

"Mm. Okay, I will be right back." I hear his footsteps fade away. Sitting there, I ponder this man and the whiplash I felt from meeting him.

We leave the Apple Store, saddled down with the new laptop, case, sleeve, and several other accessories that Maverick insisted I pick out. It makes me a little uncomfortable to think about how much money he just spent in that store, but he kept assuring me that he could afford it and wouldn't take no for an answer—in an endearing way, not a creepy one.

"Do you have anything else you need to do while we are at the mall? Or do you want me to take you home now?" Maverick asks.

I would insist I take the bus home from here, but I don't feel safe doing that with all the bags from Apple—and Maverick makes me feel safe.

"Home is fine, thanks."

We make our way back out through the car park, and I am still surprised at how well he acts as a visual aid.

"Have you spent time with a blind person before?" I ask, curious as to how he is so well-adjusted to assisting—without overwhelming—me.

"No, I have some minor experience with other disabilities. Growing up, we had a boy named Carl in our year and he had down syndrome. After a few derogative comments were made by other students, we had a disability advocate come and speak at our school. He taught us all about how just because someone is disabled and does things differently, it doesn't make *them* different. I remember one of the boys in my brothers' grade made a big deal about how it was like disabled people need to be treated a particular way because they were aliens. And for lack of a better analogy, were like someone from a different country or planet.

"The speaker then went on to say, 'You wouldn't congratulate a Russian person for moving to the United States of America and living an independent and fulfilled life. It is the same with a disabled person. You don't congratulate them for doing something for themselves. You don't tell them they are an inspiration because they are normal. You treat them as a normal person.' Now, he did go on to say that we still had to be aware and considerate of their abilities and, for example, I wouldn't throw a basketball at you without telling you it was coming first. Be considerate and aware, but not impolite and condescending."

"Wow." I am a bit speechless—I wasn't expecting that. His steps hesitate, and I notice we have arrived back at the car. Maverick leads me back to the passenger door, allowing me to sit by myself before moving to the boot to load the purchases into it. I feel the car dip as he closes the boot and comes around to enter the driver's seat.

"So, where are we headed?" Maverick asks, clipping in his seat belt.

I give him my address, and he enters it into his GPS system.

I am still processing what he said about disabled people and remain silent while he drives. After the way I have been treated in the past, I am hesitant to believe this situation. People always start of treating me 'normally', being nice and friendly. Until they start excluding me. They assume because I am vision impaired, I can't do things with them—they don't invite me to the movies, and either start treating me like an invalid, or ghost me altogether. Will Maverick be just another person who changes when I start to get attached?

"Did I upset you?" he hedges, cutting into my thoughts.

"What? No! I'm sorry, I am just processing," I reply honestly. "No one has ever spoken to me like you do—and to think that it's because teenage-Maverick actually paid attention at school and is kind and considerate…well, it's a little farfetched."

He barks out a laugh. It is husky and fills the car—enveloping me in his delight.

"I can assure you—I had my typical *teenage boy* moments too. But with my family—we've always been taught to be under-standing and helpful. My mum is a primary school teacher and ensured we were all gentlemen."

"All? How many are you?"

"Uh, five. All boys," he replies hesitantly, like this is sacred information. I sense this is a subject he doesn't want to speak about.

"Wow. It's just Taylor and me in our family. She's my older sister and my best friend." I offer to take the spotlight off him for a bit. "I suppose our childhood was just as average as everyone else's, all things considered. We grew up nearby, and my parents still live in our childhood home. We had our years of angst and drama in the household, mine fuelled even more so by overprotective parents. To this day they struggle with my independence. It took Taylor and I sitting them down together to convince them to 'allow' me to move in with Taylor. It has been easier since I moved out of home. I have more freedom and am able to manage myself, without them hovering around." I reply, surprised that I am divulging so much information to him. "Uh, sorry for the word vomit."

"It's okay. You want to talk more about it?" he asks compassionately.

"You have arrived at your destination," the GPS announces, cutting into our conversation.

"Out of time." I laugh. "Thank you so much for all that you have done for me today, Maverick."

"Will you let me help you to carry all your things inside?" I swear he sounds nervous. As if he is afraid I would say no.

"Of course. Where did you park?"

"I am in your driveway."

"Okay." I get out of the car, hoisting my bag over my shoulder and extending my cane. I make my way onto the porch and hear Maverick slam the boot shut, the gravel crunching as he follows me to the door.

Removing the house keys from my pocket, I thumb through them until I reach the correct one for the screen door, unlock it, and change keys for the wood door. Once both doors are unlocked, I swing the door wide and call out, "Tay, are you home?"

I know she is at work, so I don't know why I did it. But if I am honest with myself, there was a part of me that wanted to be alone with Maverick. I am not ready for my time with him to come to an end yet, and I am especially not ready for my sister to psychoanalyse everything that happened today.

"Do you want to come in for a bit?" I ask him. "Wait, am I holding you up? Did you have other plans this afternoon that I have just stolen you from?"

"Yes, I would like to come in, and no, you didn't steal me from anything other than completing our Finance homework."

"Ugh," I groan, stepping into the house and going through the motions of placing my bag, cane, keys, and shoes in their spots so I can find them later and not trip over items strewn around. "I hate that class. Unfortunately, it is essential for my degree."

He closes the door behind him, and I make my way into the lounge room, sitting down on the comfy couch. It dips as he sits down next to me, and presumably sets my new equipment on the coffee table, if I am placing the sound right.

"Me too."

"What are you majoring in?" I ask, surprised this didn't come up earlier today.

"Boring old Business Management. You?"

"Major in Business Management with a minor in Music Studies."

"Music Studies? Do you play?" he asks excitedly.

"No, I wish, but I was never able to pick it up. A friend in high school tried to teach me, let me just say—a scratched record sounds better than me." His laugh washes over me. "I want to become a producer or talent recruiter. Finding people who have the skill to make it big and getting that happen for them and helping them get the sound just right."

"You really love music," he muses.

"I do. I know I said it before, but it makes me feel approachable. And wearing band merch or covering my belongings in stickers is another part of that. Plus, it's a talking point. Someone can see my shirt and be all, 'Oh, I like them too!' and the whole conversation just goes smoother because they have something in common with me. It gives me a few minutes before they realise I am blind and start treating me strangely. Some people talk to me like I am uneducated or a child, or ask me *really* invasive questions." I chuckle awkwardly.

"Oh shit!"

"What?"

"Your stickers!"

"Huh?"

"Your MacBook that we replaced was covered in stickers. You lost them all." He sounds so concerned, something in me reaches out for him, needing to soothe and comfort him.

"Oh!" I chuckle. "It's not that big a deal—I have a lot more."

"Are you sure? I can get you more, replace the ones you lost because of me."

"No, seriously, it's fine. If I showed you my room, you would understand."

"Okay," he replies, the couch shifting as he stands.

"Okay what?" I ask, perplexed.

"Show me your room so I can understand," Maverick says, excitement ringing in his voice.

"What?" I laugh. "You can't be serious."

"Hey, you offered. I am only accepting. I want to see what other bands you are into, Cecilia." He sings my name like the song. Strangely, it doesn't annoy me like it does when Taylor does it.

"Okay," I say, planning to call him out on his bluff. Surely, he doesn't actually want to come and see my room. He only met me today—even with how flirty we have both been, he has to know nothing could happen. Right?

I make my way back through the house, not needing my cane as I know where everything is—the benefits of muscle memory and living in the same house for three years. Our house is pretty basic: one bathroom, single-story, three bedrooms with open-plan living and dining.

"This is it!" I proclaim, pushing open my bedroom door and stepping into the room. This is the first time a boy has ever been in my room—in any of my rooms. When I lived with my parents, there was a strict no-boys-in-the-bedroom rule for my friends. I sense him step into the room and hover behind me, his heated breath blooming against the side of my head.

My pulse spikes. What is he thinking? I know my room is covered with Fly By posters and a few other artists like the Foo Fighters, Harry Styles, Katy Perry, and Miley Cyrus.

"So, what do you think?" I ask after a few minutes of silence.

"You're right. You have the merch side of things covered." Maverick chuckles close to my ear.

I smile sheepishly, and I swear I don't lean into him. Not even a little bit. "Yeah, Taylor is always a big help in getting the right things in the right spots. I know I can't see it, but I still like having it around me. You know?"

"Yeah, C, I get it," he murmurs softly. I can tell he is staring down at me now, and a blush rises up from my chest and heats my face.

Needing a topic change, I stammer out, "D-do you want to say for dinner?"

"With your sister?" he asks after a small pause.

"No, she is working late tonight. I am going to order in if you want to join me?" I offer. Is it risky telling this practical stranger that I will be alone for a while? I don't know, and I don't know if I care at this point.

I am not afraid of him. Nothing he has done or said gives me any kind of "creeper vibes," as Taylor so lovingly calls it. And if I am being honest with myself, I don't want him to be a stranger anymore. I want the chance to get to know him.

"Yeah, I would love to stay," Maverick replies, his voice and words warming my insides.

Seven - Maverick

I SHOULDN'T BE DOING this. I should tell her who I am. I should leave. I shouldn't be here in her house, alone with her, when all I can think about is twisting my hand in those vibrant red strands, pushing her against a wall, and claiming her mouth in a kiss. I feel my cock stiffen in my jeans at the thought—talk about inappropriate thoughts at inopportune times.

I want to stay in her room, but I know how dangerous that could be.

"So, what do you want to order for dinner?" I ask her as we leave her room.

"I was planning on getting pizza. Pizza is my favourite food group."

"Food group?"

"Yup. It needs its own food group. There are so many different kinds of pizza, and you can eat it at any time of the day."

This woman is just full of surprises.

"What's your favourite pizza?" I ask her, finding it's something I suddenly need to know. I need every drop of information I can get out of her before our time is up, because I know it will come to an end—either when she finds out that I have been keeping the truth from her or when I stick to my plan and never talk to her again after today. It's what I should do. I should leave now. I shouldn't follow her back out to the living room, watching her luscious locks sway as she walks. Or how her ass looks in those tight jeans. I am jealous of those jeans and how close they get to be to her.

No. I shouldn't be doing that.

"Hawaiian," she responds sternly, as if expecting me to disagree.

"Hawaiian is definitely the best," I confirm.

"Oh my gosh! You really think so? Taylor hates it. She is one of those 'pineapple doesn't belong on pizza' heathens."

I laugh as she pulls her iPhone from her pocket and navigates through the options of ordering two Hawaiian pizzas to be delivered.

"I'm sorry, I should have already offered. Did you want something to drink?"

"Sure. Just water is fine, C."

She stands from the couch, collecting us both a cold bottle of water from the fridge before sitting next to me.

"So, tell me about you, Maverick," Cecilia commands.

"What do you want to know?" I feel like I am taking a polygraph. I have been careful with what I have told her so far. She said she has been a fan of Fly By since the beginning. If I tell her too much, she might start to figure it out.

"What do you like to do in your spare time?"

I thought about that for a minute. I don't want this day to feel cheap, and even though I am lying and keeping a part of me a secret…maybe I can show her the other part of me. The part the media and public doesn't get to see.

"Uh, I am going to lose a few cool points for admitting to this —and if you ever tell anyone, I will deny it. But I love anything romance. Chick-flick movies, romance novels, rom-coms, anything really."

"You're pulling my leg." She giggles.

"Am not. I swear on my life, that's what I like to do." Admitting this to her feels like a weight off my shoulders—like I am finally being myself.

"What's your favourite?"

"Movie would have to be *You've Got Mail*."

She breaks out laughing again. "I'm sorry, but oh my god, you aren't real. I swear I am about to wake up still on the floor of the courtyard and realise this has all been a dream."

"Are you calling me dreamy? Dreamy like Mr. Darcy, or dreamy like Westley?" I ask, showing her truly how much of a romance fiend I am. It feels good making her laugh and being this open with someone who isn't my family.

"Oh no, Maverick, you are a character all on your own. I don't think they would compare to you."

"Oh, really?" Shit, I am flirting again. I shouldn't be—but fuck if it doesn't feel right. I want to tell her that technically, I am named after a character, but that would give too much away. She is a Fly By fan; she would know the story behind our names.

While we wait for the pizza to arrive, we discuss more books that we've both read—Cecilia listens to audiobooks, or her family takes turns reading some aloud to her if there isn't an audiobook available.

"I can resort to Voice Over for eBooks or scanned books, but the robot voice and mispronunciation really ruin the experience for me." Cecilia said, "And Braille books are too expensive, and we could never afford them, plus they are hard to transport around if I want to read while on the bus, or between classes."

We had a lot of favourites in common and moved from books back to music, and then to discussing our professors. When the pizza arrived, I brought the box inside, and we grabbed ourselves pieces.

"I am not sure if this is rude to ask, and please don't feel you have to answer. You can tell me off if you want to," I start between mouthfuls of pizza. "God, this is going to sound bad. Have you always been blind? How—how blind are you? God, I was right, that sounds awful. I am so sorry."

She chuckles softly. "Yes, I was born blind. Everyone is different; there isn't like seeing and not seeing. There are varying degrees of low vision and blindness. For me, I am hypersensitive to light and can see shadows sometimes. It really depends on how bright the room—or space—is, and what my eyes or brain feel like doing that day."

"That's why you wear the sunglasses when you are outside... because of the light?"

She nods while taking another bite of her pizza. "Sometimes I get really bad headaches if the lights are too intense, so it's easier to be preventive and wear the glasses to ensure I don't get them."

"There are so many things that I never considered. I had a thought earlier, is it offensive for me to use words like 'see' and 'look' when talking with you?"

"No, it isn't, they are relative words, and it would be more offensive to limit your vocabulary to speak with me."

"Does that happen often?"

"Yes, some people overcompensate and are too helpful or selective with their words. It reinforces how people treat me differently."

"Wow, I didn't realise people could be so inconsiderate."

"You aren't the first. I had a bit of a rough upbringing. My family is great—but kids are cruel. I was picked on for being poor, shy and F different, and for a while I really struggled between wanting to fit in like a 'normal' kid and between being true to myself. After some counselling, I eventually got to a place where I accepted that I couldn't control other people. But I could control my reaction to them."

"I think it's cool that you dealt with bullying like that. I'm not sure I'd be that mature. I don't know many teenagers who would take that approach to bullying and harassment."

She smiles softly at me, a hint of pizza sauce staining the corner of her lips. Without thinking, I reach out and swipe the pad of my thumb across the sauce and—my body acting independently of my mind—put my thumb in my mouth, tasting the sauce.

"Uh—" I freeze, my mind catching up. "I'm sorry, I shouldn't have done that."

"It's okay." Cecilia blushes, ducking her head and pushing a lock of hair behind her ear. My blood pulses, heading straight to my cock.

"I should go," I burst out, my nerves too on-edge from being around this temptress for so long. I jump to my feet.

"Yeah, okay," she says softly, and something inside me cracks at the disheartened tone in her voice. "I've kept you long enough... you should go before Taylor gets home, or I will never hear the end of it." She laughs, clearly trying to conceal her emotions.

"Is it okay if I hug you?" I say before my mind catches up with me. My body craves to touch her, but that is a really bad idea with the situation in my pants.

Seemingly shocked again, she nods. She stands up and holds out her arms awkwardly.

I need this. *Just one hug*, I tell myself. Just to feel her body pressed against mine to round out today before I let her go and leave her alone.

Without hesitating, I step into her embrace and wrap my arms around her small frame. My nose lands in her soft hair, and a sigh escapes me as I feel her hands slide up my back, pressing in against the dip of my spine and rolling over my shoulders.

A shiver racks her body, and I feel my cock harden more at her reaction to me and having her body pressed against mine. Pulling back, she trails her hands across my waist and up and over my chest. Her fingertips draw up the side of my neck, scratching my short beard as she cups my jaw. Tension bubbles between us. I stare down, watching her thoughts flicker across her face. Her tongue darts out to lick her lips—watching her bite down on the corner of her lips, my cock leaking precum in my briefs. Before I can stop myself or tell myself how bad an idea this is, I launch forward, pushing my lips against her mouth in a soft, intense kiss.

Her lips mould against mine—plush and soft, a small gasp escaping her. I place my hands on her waist, enjoying the sweet taste of pineapple and something that is uniquely Cecilia. I will never be able to eat Hawaiian pizza again without thinking of her and getting a hard-on. I sneak my tongue out and groan as she grants me access to her mouth.

Our tongues tangle, twisting as I suck lightly on hers. A groan rumbles out of me and her fingers thread through my hair, holding me against her. Cecilia kisses me back with an intensity I crave. Her tongue plays with mine as I smooth my hands around to her lower back—fingertips brushing against the top of her magnificent ass. I pull back slightly, biting down on her lower lip, causing her to whimper in need.

Her hands tighten in my hair, pulling my face back down, and this time she kisses me first. Leaving one hand in my hair, her other drops to my chest and spreads out over my pecs. Cecilia moans into my mouth, and I drink it down. I have never felt a passion, a heat, a need like this. Her hand roams my torso, trailing over my nipple and dipping down to caress my abs.

I tense at her touch, at war with myself. There is no denying how much I want to have her writhing underneath me as I pound into her, her bright red hair fanning out across her pillow. She cannot be just another one-night stand, though. Emotionally, I cannot handle it—but how can there be anything more with Cecilia? She is a superfan who is going to freak out the moment that she realises who I am. She will never want *me*—never see me for who I am. I will just be the Mav from Fly By to her, like I am to everyone.

With that sad realisation, I tear my lips away from her—wishing I could stay here forever with her as her Maverick, the real Maverick that she deserves the chance to get to know and be with. But that's just not in the cards for us.

"I'm sorry, I shouldn't have done that," I whisper, bittersweet joy brimming at my edges.

"W-wha—?" Cecilia replies, dazed and still recovering from our kiss.

"I need to go." I detangle myself from her gently. "I'm sorry, C. You—you don't know what today means to me."

Forcing myself, I gather my keys and head to her door.

"Wait, Maverick, wait, please," Cecilia begs, breaking my heart as I leave her house—and her life.

Eight - Cecilia

THE SOUND of the door slamming shut reverberates through me.

Maverick's gone. He kissed me and just left. His last words bounce around my mind. *I'm sorry, C. You—you don't know what today means to me.*

He's *sorry*? Sorry for kissing me? Well, isn't that just a punch in the gut. The first guy to ever make me feel this way—to ever kiss me, even—is sorry that he did it.

I don't have enough time to figure out if I am hurt or angry when I hear the door opening again.

"Maverick?" Did he come back already?

"No, it's Taylor," my sister replies, her light footsteps carrying her into the lounge room with me. I realise I am still standing there, mouth agape, trying to recover from the magical crazy that was the last six or so hours of my life. "Why were you expecting Maverick?" she asks coyly.

"N-no reason," I stutter out, sinking to sit on the couch, tears stinging the back of my eyes.

"Mmhmm, and that's not beard burn on your cheeks."

"What?" I screech, causing Taylor to laugh.

"You don't actually have beard burn, but that does confirm my suspicions about a good night kiss."

"Oh, Taylor," I whine, "it was more than that. It was stupendous."

"That's a big word."

"I can't think of anything else to explain it. I told you on the phone that he was going to pay to fix my MacBook screen, right?"

"Yes, but looking at the coffee table, I am assuming he bought more than that."

"Well, my MacBook was too old, and they no longer had the screens to repair mine. So he made the sales lady come over with the newest model and show me how it works and all the changes since my Mac, confirmed that I liked it, then bought it and a handful of other things he insisted I needed."

"Whoa."

"Then he stayed with me in the store for the half hour it took for the sales lady to transfer over all my data to the new computer and sync it to my iPhone and watch. At no point was he frustrated with how long it took me to get a handle on everything. Then when we got home, he was upset when he realised I lost all the stickers on my old Mac."

"Really?"

Nodding, I add, "Then he joined me here for dinner before kissing me, Tay. He kissed me! Can you believe it!" I sigh like a typical teenager when their crush notices them for the first time.

"I can believe it," Tay says excitedly. "I knew this was your meet-cute moment!"

"No, no, none of that! I will not have you twisting my mind with your happily-ever-after nonsense. You know as well as I do that a guy like that probably kissed me out of pity. He wouldn't want to be with me. He basically peeled me off him, apologised, and ran out of here. He didn't even take my number. I will probably never hear from him again."

"Don't say things like that! He went out of his way to spend time with you today. He could have just given you money for a new screen or computer. He could have just ordered one online and had it delivered here. He didn't have to come into the house and eat dinner with you. And he kissed you—you said he started it. He definitely wanted you."

"You really think so?" I ask, ashamed of the hope in my voice.

"Yes, honey, I do. Probably was just freaked out that I was coming home. How was he with the whole blind thing?"

I bark out a laugh. My sister is nothing if not direct. I recap for her how he bowled me over in the courtyard, and the courtesy he treated me with for the rest of the day.

"Tay, he didn't treat me like a freak or an invalid. To him, I was just a regular person, with a different barrier to over-come." His words come back to me: *Just because someone is disabled and does things differently, it doesn't make them different.*

"Man, I wish I had gotten here earlier to get a look at him."

"Oh, Taylor, he is amazing. Absolutely ripped torso—I could feel his abs and the dip in his spine through his shirt—and this short beard with hair that I could just run my hands through for hours."

"Tall?"

"Oh, his chin hits my head just."

"Wow, Cece! Sounds like you landed yourself a catch."

"I hope so." I sigh again, reminding myself that even if he did rush out of here, his kiss was not something I would forget in a heartbeat.

Nine - Maverick

I CAN'T GET Cecilia off my mind. No one has ever stuck in my mind like this, and I only met C yesterday.

I promised myself that I would keep my distance, but there is this niggling feeling in my head that I need to do something for her. Without any hesitation, I call our manager.

"Mitch?" I say when he answers the phone.

"Hey Mav, how's it hanging?" His voice echoes through the phone.

"Yeah mate, it's alright. I need you to do something for me."

"Shoot."

This is one of the things I love about Mitch: he's direct and doesn't fuck around. We picked him up shortly after we won *What It Takes!* and he has been a blessing, keeping us all in check and ensuring we get what is best, not just for us, but for our mentality.

"I need you to send me over a bunch of our stickers—everything we got from different concerts, songs, albums, our logo, everything."

"Oookay. Am I allowed to ask why?"

"Nope," I reply bluntly, popping the *p*.

"Mmhmm. How many do you want?"

"At least fifty. And I need you to do something special too," I say as a new idea hits me, "I would like a few ones made that are like 3D or embossed—whatever—where you can feel our signatures and our logo. Is that something you can do?"

"Yeah, man. I will get you fancy embossed-whatever stickers," he answers with a bit of a laugh.

"Good, get it to me ASAP," I say before hanging up the phone. I know I won't live this down, but at this point, I don't care. I want Cecilia to have something that she loves, and as evidenced by her room, band merch is a good start.

In classic Mitch fashion, all the stickers are delivered to my place the next day. Placing them all in a box with a note, I drop them off at Cecilia's place. I am tempted to knock to see her and hand them off, but if she answers, there is no way that I wouldn't kiss her—and I can't do that again, no matter how much I want to.

I wish I could be there when she opens the box with her sister to see her reaction. Would she be happy to hear from me?

Would she do the math and start to figure out who I am? I look down at the note I have taped to the top of the box.

Cecilia,

I hope you are enjoying the laptop. Please accept these stickers in replacement of the ones I caused you to lose. I know you said you had enough, but I wanted to do something special for you.

I'm sorry for everything.

Yours,

Maverick.

The "yours" might be a bit much, but no matter how I try and convince myself, I know in this moment it is true. She has a hold on me, and I hope that I can break it before it breaks me.

I surprise Professor Jones by being the first to class—which is extremely rare for me—but I need to stake out a spot where I can be close to her. I move to the seat behind and two down from Cecilia's normal chair, giving me a view of the door and the students arriving.

My toes tap out a beat, and anxiety wracks me. It's been a week since we met, and I've only seen her once since then, on Wednesday when we had class together. I sat at the back of the room then, thinking it would be easier. Newsflash: it wasn't. Hence why I am now counting the seconds and sitting as close as I can justify.

My heartbeat picks up as I see her enter the room. I watch as she walks toward me, that bright hair flaming around her, hypnotising me. I force myself to remain seated and not rush to her to touch and caress her. To hear her beautiful voice say my name—say anything.

A smile tugs at the corner of my mouth as I see her new MacBook covered with so many Fly By stickers you can't see what colour the computer is. She trails her fingers over one in particular, and I wonder which one it is. Which one has become her favourite? I itch to ask her, to know more peculiar facts about her that no one else knows.

Fuck.

This is the opposite of what I need to be doing right now. I should've sat in a different seat. I have the perfect view of her profile, and I spend the next two hours forcing myself to pay attention to Finance and stealing glances at Cecilia. Thank god it's Friday.

The second Professor Jones releases the class, I am out of my seat and out of the room. If I stay any longer, I'll cave and go to her. Needing to escape the city, I decide to go to Mum and Dad's early, driving up there tonight. Hopefully, a weekend in a different city from Cecilia will help me shake her from my mind.

This obsession I have with her is edging on creepy—I do feel possessive about her, and I know I shouldn't. This has to be a cruel trick of fate, to give me this opportunity to know an amazing woman and not be allowed to be with her.

A voice niggles at the back of my mind before I can block it out. *You're the only one saying you can't be with her.*

I can't. I've read that book, seen that movie, I know how it ends—and it's not a happy ending for me.

You don't get with groupies or megafans. It's prenups to make sure I don't get ruined. It's NDAs to ensure my girlfriend doesn't air our dirty laundry to the media for the biggest payout. It's a child born to control and manipulate you. There's too much drama.

You don't know that Cecilia will be like that. You could get to know her as Maverick and not tell her that you are the Mav.

My inner cynic and inner romantic are at war as I drive out to Mum and Dad's, hoping that this is my chance at finding *the One* but knowing that isn't reality. I'm a romantic at heart—the main reason I love romance novels and movies. How can you not be a romantic with my family? Mum and Dad are literally childhood sweethearts, boy-and-girl-next-door, and best friends-to-lovers tropes. I grew up thinking that was normal. It wasn't until we made it big that I realised that—unfortunately—their happy marriage is an anomaly. Not everyone is as lucky as our parents, and as the years went on, hook-up after hook-up, one-night stand after one-night stand, I began to lose hope that I would ever find my real-life romance story.

Cecilia couldn't be that for me. There is too much at risk. It's not worth the pain of rejection when she turns me down. I have been hurt too many times now, and I just can't put my heart on the line again.

I park on the curb and exit my car, looking up at the house that started it all for us. Would I have still met Cecilia if we hadn't won *What It Takes!*?

Before I have the chance to overthink it, Mum opens the door and steps out onto the porch, looking quintessentially herself: white linen pants, bright blue tank top, and her hair out and wild. Peace rushes through me as I walk toward her.

"Mav, are you okay?" Her soft voice washes over me, further soothing my frayed nerves.

"Yeah, Ma. I just needed to get away from everything for a few days."

She purses her lips, looking me over. "Are you sure?"

Damn her and her ability to read her children.

"Not now, Ma, please?"

"Only if you will tell me what's wrong before you go home."

"Ugh, fine," I relent. Sometimes it's easier to just give into her. "Is anyone else here?" I ask, giving her a long hug. Long because Mum won't release me.

"Just Ethan. Your father is still at work."

"Ah, can you let me go now?"

"Not just yet. I need my baby," she replies, giving me the ability to take in her affection without shame.

When she steps back, my shoulders slump. I know by the look on her face I won't be able to get away with lying to her.

"Is it okay if I go into the garage?"

"Okay, baby. Want me to send Ethan in?"

"Maybe later, I wanna be alone for a little bit."

"Okay," she replies, concern edging her voice.

I follow her into the house, retreating into the garage before Ethan can see me. Looking around the space, I notice all the changes we've made over since we took over the garage. Walls that were originally full of shelves and a bunch of old toys and clothes are now covered in soundproofing. We each have a station full of equipment, extra picks, drumsticks, leads, and instruments. I walk over to my guitar rack, picking up my acoustic Fender. My fingers itching to play and my mind needing the distraction, I start strumming through random songs.

I play some of our songs, each flowing into the next, and then slip into covers of popular songs. Before I know what I am doing, I am halfway through playing "Oh Cecilia" by The Vamps. Even here she floods my mind. My mind snags on the lyrics again, paying more attention to them now.

Although we're many miles apart but I still feel her

There'll never be another one like my Cecilia

Oh where, oh where could she be?

Does she still care about me?

When will she finally come back to, come back to me?

Could that be any more fucking relatable? It's spooky how similar this song is to our—my—situation. Maybe The Vamps are psychic, or time travellers. That makes the most sense.

"Okay, I think even you have had enough moping time. What's going on?" Ethan asks, leaning against the garage door.

"You wouldn't get it."

"Because I'm soooo young? Please, Mav, I'm almost eighteen."

"I know. A baby." Stirring up my brothers has always been my favourite pastime.

"Very funny. I'm not letting you change the subject. What's wrong? Or do I need to call a brother meeting?"

"Nah, man, not a brother meeting."

A brother meeting was something we implemented when we got famous. As the title implies, it is a gathering of all five of us to discuss the shit in our lives without judgement or complaints. We needed it on tour to get over the issues we were having within the band, like tight living arrangements and the high demand of the industry.

"Too late!" Charlie and Joel singsong as they saunter in from the house.

"Sorry, bro. When you mope—you mope hard. And that calls for all of us," Tom says, following them into the garage.

How long must I have been here playing for them all to be here already? An hour? Two?

"I'm not moping, and I don't need a brother meeting." Even though I don't need this, I am comforted to know that they have my back and support me no matter what.

"Well, Mum called us, so clearly you do," Charlie says.

"Mum called a brother meeting?" I ask, shaking my head. That woman. She always knows what her kids need. Maybe I do need this.

"Yup. Soooo spill!" Tom says, his voice mocking a teenage gossip.

There was no getting out of this now.

"Uh"—I heave out a breath— "I met a girl."

"Oooh! Scandalous!" Ethan mocks.

"She's different!" I protest, showing my hand way too early.

"So what's the issue? She doesn't want you?" Joel asks.

"She is a megafan," I reply.

"Oh, so she went crazy on you?" Charlie asks.

"She doesn't know who I am."

"Well, she clearly isn't much of a fan, then. I am still not seeing the issue here. So—you bang her like you do everyone else, what's the big deal?" Joel asks.

"Hey!" I shout.

"Wait, this is about you wanting more than just a fuck with her, isn't it?" Ethan interjects.

"Don't let Mum catch you saying that," I scold him.

"She knows, and she is okay with it. I may be seventeen, but I am a rock star; occasionally I say *fuck*. You usually are okay with it, too, when you aren't trying to change the topic. So, answer the fucking question," Ethan replies, slapping the back of my head like I am an idiot. And to be fair, I am.

"I want more with her, yeah." I start talking and can't help myself. These are my brothers—they won't judge me, and they'll understand. "But it can't happen. You guys have seen what it's like when you get involved with a fan. There is too much drama. And to be fucking honest with you, I'm terrified of her rejection. What if she only wants a night with me like everyone else? I want to be more to Cecilia—to be everything, and that's fucking insane since I've only spent a handful of hours with her and kissed her once." I hang my head, my chest twisting with all the what if's running around my head.

"You said she's different?" Joel asks.

"She's amazing, man," I gush like a pubescent teen. "Fiery red hair, green eyes, knows all about music. Wants to be a producer and help the little guy develop their sound. Has followed us since the talent show. Only one thing wrong with her," I mutter at the end.

"What's that?" they all ask at once. We all laugh, and Charlie and Ethan call out "JINX!"

Ignoring them, I continue, "Fucking Joel's her favourite—she thinks he's the most emotionally in touch."

"Score!" Joel calls out, punching his fist in the air. "I'll bag this Sylvia chick, then."

"The fuck you will!" I growl, standing and placing my guitar on the floor—I fucking never put it on the floor, but clearly my brother needed a lesson in what doesn't belong to him.

"Possessive, are we?" Joel singsongs, his mouth tipped up in a smirk, and I realise this is what he was hoping for. Egging me on to raise a reaction out of me.

"Asshole!" I grumble, sitting back down and picking up my guitar again. "You made me put Josie on the ground, you dick!" Yeah, I named my guitar. They all have names; they're my girls. It's a musician thing. Some people don't get it.

"It answers the question, though," Tom says.

"What question?" I ask. I really don't understand what they're talking about.

"Whether you should go after her or not," Tom replies.

"I'm not going after her," I reply, determined.

"That's bullshit and we all know it," Charlie replies. "It's really only a matter of time now."

"You guys know how I am—you know how long I have wanted a love like Mum and Dad's, no matter how hard I try to deny it. I have had too many false starts, and I think it's just time to accept that it's not going to happen to me."

"Are you lying to yourself too? Or just us?" Joel asks. "You are the biggest romantic I know. You know how these things work.

If your life was one of those sex novels you read, do you really think you aren't meant to be? Tell me, why are you so hung up on her? Great looks and music taste aside. What did you guys do? Did you already fuck, and you don't know how to go back for more?"

"Fuck off, idiot, she isn't like that. She *is* more. I broke her computer, so I took her to the store to fix it and ended up getting her a new one and a bunch of extra shit to ensure the next person who runs into her won't break it. She relies on it for school and doesn't have any spare money floating around. Then I helped her carry all her shit into her house. We just hung out, eating pizza on her couch and talking. And maybe kissed a little bit. But I left before anything more could happen.

"She doesn't know that I am *the* Maverick from her beloved Fly By," I went on. "I had so many chances to tell her when we were together—she talked about us a lot, guys." I chuckle at the memory. "How can I just go up to her now after ghosting her for over a week? She'll have the shits, and if she doesn't, she will once she finds out I have been keeping things from her. The best thing is for me to just keep my distance, I'll move on from her eventually. It was only a kiss."

My brothers exchanged a few looks.

"Okay, Mav," Ethan replies, breaking the awkward silence that followed my word vomit. "You keep telling yourself that. I, for one, cannot wait until we finally meet her and get to tell her all about your tantrum." He laughs and moves to his keys, and the others all drift toward their instruments as well.

Ethan starts playing the chords for "Inverted," and I immediately think of Cecilia. She is right. It's totally a sex song. When we wrote it, we were immature horny teenagers and thought blatant, in-your-face sex references were so cool and unique.

Taking a deep breath, I stand and swap Josie out for Clara, my Fender Stratocaster. (I have a thing for Fenders, obviously.) Returning to my seat, I start playing along with Ethan—Tom and Charlie joining in on their count before Joel starts singing.

I lose myself in the melody, playing along with my brothers. Soon this song will be normal to me again, and I will no longer have Cecilia in my head. My gut twists at the thought, but I know it's what is best. Best to protect my heart from her grasp.

I'd like to say I am strong enough to stay away from her. I'd like to think that I will finish my moping and move on.

But that won't happen.

Ten - Cecilia

HOW STUPID DOES he think I am? I thought he was different. Just like everyone else, he thinks, *She's blind so she won't know.*

Of course I noticed that he sat near me in class for the last three weeks. He chose seats closer and closer to me every lesson, and now he is sitting next to me. I can feel his eyes as he stares at me while I try to focus on the professor. I can smell his cologne, a mix of leather and citrus. You wouldn't think it works, but it is the most intoxicating smell—perhaps ever.

And yet, those stickers.

Taylor looked up those 3D ones online, but she couldn't find them anywhere. He must have had them custom-made. Those pesky stickers showed he *had* thought about me, had cared.

Taylor was thrilled by this whole thing and kept speculating about how he loved me and we were destined to be together. I tried my hardest to not fall into her rose-tinted visions, but those stickers and that kiss had me fantasizing about what it would be like if he loved me.

Honestly, at first, I thought he wasn't real—a dream conjured to make myself feel better. But no, he is real. The thought of him turns to anger, boiling in the pit of my stomach. Despite being so close, he never talks to me. My only guess is that he kissed me out of pity and has regretted it. I feel his gaze on me —again. He thinks he can just kiss me, leave, then ignore me for three weeks while staring at me and not have to deal with my wrath? He is sorely mistaken.

Narrowing my eyes, I give him the most pissed-off glare I can manage.

"You and I need to talk after class. Not an option," I murmur to not interrupt the professor.

I hear his breath hitch. "Fuck," he whispers to himself.

The rest of the lesson is a blur as I mull over what I am going to say to him. Once we are dismissed, Maverick remains in his seat, waiting to take his cue from me. I rise from my seat after packing up my bag, extending my cane and placing my sunglasses on my face. I am going to need all the armour I can get for this conversation. I'm not sure where to have this conversation, but I sure do not want to have it in front of our professor.

"We can walk and talk," I say, turning and walking towards the door. I hear his footsteps as he falls in line behind me, following me silently out of the room. "Why?" I ask bluntly.

"Why what?" Maverick's deep voice rushes over me. My cheeks heat. I hadn't realised exactly how much I had missed the sound of his voice. Which is just stupid.

"Why everything, Maverick. Why run out of my house? Why send me a gift? Why not talk to me for three weeks but sit near me in class and stare at me all day?"

"I don't stare at you." He didn't deny the rest of it, though.

"I know you do—just tell me why!"

"I don't know what you are talking about."

"'Yours, Maverick.' Did you not write those words on the box you left on my porch?"

"Uh—"

"And about that—some of those were custom-made. Where did you—you know, that's not important right now. You need to leave me alone, Maverick."

"L-leave you alone?"

"Yes. I have had enough of you staring at me and disrupting my day."

"But—I—"

"But what, Maverick? You have done a semi-decent job keeping away from me for the last few weeks, and I get it, okay? You spent time with me out of pity, but I don't need that from you. From anyone," I spit out, anger coiling in my gut.

"I don't pity you. I didn't hang out with you because I *pity* you!" He spits the word like it offends him. "It's not you."

"Oh, really. Wow, we aren't even dating, and you are giving me the 'it's not you, it's me' line?" I start walking faster. I know I started this conversation, but I need to get away from it— like, now. I'm anxious to be away from his intoxicating presence. "You are just like everyone else, changing how you treat me—ghosting me."

"It's not a line. I am not good enough for you. My life is a mess, and there are things I need to tell you."

"Why?"

"Why am I not good enough for you?" He asks, confused.

"No." I hide a smirk, angry that he causes this reaction in me. "Why do you need to tell me something? You have proven over the last few weeks that I am nothing to you. So, clearly, I don't need to know."

"Please—I need to tell you!"

"No, you don't."

"Why?"

"Because I don't want to hear it."

He remains silent for a heartbeat, continuing to walk in step with me. We are almost at the bus stop now, where I can get clear of him and this conversation.

"Okay, I won't tell you now—but one day, you will need to hear it. I haven't been able to get you off my mind, C. And quite frankly, I don't want to anymore. I thought it would be better for you if I kept my distance. You don't need me or my drama in your life, but you have ensnared me and I'm not sure if I want you to let me go. Please let me make this up to you. Give me a fresh start?"

"Why should I?"

"Don't you feel what's between us?"

"I thought I did, until you avoided me for weeks," I hiss.

"Yeah, okay, I deserved that," he replies, subdued. "Will you at least let me drive you home so we can talk? Please?"

"Why? What's changed?" I whirl around, facing him, anger radiating off me. "You made it clear you don't want me, why drag it out?"

"Cecilia, that's not true. You have no idea how much I want you," he almost whispers. "Please, baby, please let me take you home."

"Why?" I ask again.

"Please? We can talk about it more in the car."

"Ugh. Fine," I harrumph unattractively. This man has my stomach in knots again.

"Can I lead you?" he asks gently, pleading with me.

"Yes," I answer while holding my hand out to take his arm.

He leads me as he did in the car park that day, politely pointing out any possible issues for me before opening the car door for me and letting me ease myself in.

The moment the door closes behind me, the overwhelming smell of leather and citrus that I associate with Maverick wracks my body, making me feel heady.

How did we go from me confronting him about practically stalking me to me getting in his car?

What have I agreed to?

Eleven - Maverick

I DON'T KNOW how I got her to agree to let me drive her home, but I am not going to mess up this chance again.

After my—for lack of a better word—*breakdown*, my resolve to stay away from her lasted all of a week. The first time I saw her again, I knew I was kidding myself. There was no way I could resist the pull she has on me.

I thought that existing within her space would be enough, and it was… just. I still craved her. I spent class staring at her longingly, wishing that we could be different, wishing that I could be brave enough to be with her and strong enough to stay away for her.

I can't believe she called me on my shit. Well, I can believe it. From the little I know of her, she is the type who would confront someone who has an issue with her. But it has been so long since anyone outside of my family was straight with me. I've never been more turned on than standing in a carpark, her yelling at me for treating her like shit. No matter what I tried telling myself, she's right. I was an absolute dick to her.

"You remember where I live, I am assuming?" Cecilia says into the silence of the car.

"Um—yeah." That's not too creepy, right?

We lapse into silence again, and even though I was the one who begged her to get in my car, I have no idea what to say now. Maybe this doesn't have to be what I dreaded. Maybe if I get her to see me for who I am as Maverick before I tell her I am the Mav of Fly By, we will have a shot at making it last.

If she falls for who I am, then I can tell her.

"So, how have the last few weeks been for you?" I ask, this new plan easing my nerves.

"Fine, I suppose. Nothing exciting or crazy has happened, other than this weird guy in glass who keeps staring at me," she replies jokingly, causing me to blush. "What about you?"

"Other than not doing a good job of concealing my affections for this amazing, gorgeous redhead in my class, not a lot. Some pining, you know, the usual," I reply, trying—and failing —to keep my voice blasé.

Cecilia chuckles, and a weight lifts off my chest. Maybe I can do this. I keep sneaking glances at her as I drive. My gut twists as I realise she is wearing a Fly By shirt again.

You can do this! I remind myself.

"I didn't think of how my actions would affect you," I start, being as honest as I can right now. "I have a lot of baggage, and I didn't want to drag you into all my drama. You deserve more than that. I didn't know how to tell you, and I figured you wouldn't be that attached to me. I am sorry, Cecilia."

"Okay. I believe you."

Phew.

"But I am not saying I understand why you thought it was best to ignore me."

"One day you will, I hope. I really am sorry."

"I hope so too, Maverick."

"So, heard any good music lately?" I ask, diving into a topic we are both comfortable with.

We spend the rest of the drive discussing new songs that have hit the charts and music industry news from the last few weeks.

I pull into her driveway and hesitate. I don't want this to be over. I want to spend more time with her—she is intoxicating.

"Are you free tomorrow?" I ask cautiously.

"Depends… why?"

"Would you like to go out on a date with me?" I close my eyes, waiting for her response. I am too scared to look at her. What if my disappearing act over the last few weeks has blown my chances with her? What if this lift home is just to placate me, and she isn't actually interested?

"Will it take you another three weeks to talk to me afterwards?" Her soft voice breaks through my wandering mind.

"No!" I laugh. "I promise that is done with."

"Okay then."

"Really?" I ask, like a kid who just found out Christmas existed.

"I am not one to hold a grudge, really, but I won't be treated like that again. This is another chance because I really think there can be something here. You better not fuck up again."

"I won't."

"Good. Where should I meet you and when?"

"I'll pick you up here at eleven?"

"Sounds great." She opens her door and turns back to me. "Do I need to dress a particular way? What are we doing?"

"We'll do lunch, and maybe something else if I can get it organised. Just wear whatever you're comfortable in, and I will look after everything else."

My mind is racing with so many options that I could do for our first official date. Cecilia starts to leave the car and pulls me out of my racing thoughts again.

"Wait," I say hastily, "can I get your phone number?"

Cecilia laughs. "I thought you'd never ask."

I program her number into my phone and send her a message so she can contact me. Her watch reads out my message.

Unknown Sender:

You are beautiful, Cecilia.

Your Maverick.

She blushes, and I reach for her hand, bring it to my lips, and place a soft kiss in the centre of her palm.

"Until tomorrow, Cecilia," I murmur into her hand before letting it drop and watching her silently leave the car. I wait for her to safely enter her house before backing out of her driveway.

I have been awake since the crack of dawn, too on edge to sleep any longer, and I am here half an hour early. I am an idiot, I know. It's just a date. I have been on plenty of dates; this should be a cakewalk.

But it's my first real date as Maverick and not the Mav in four years.

I brush my sweaty palms down my jeans again, trying to dry them before I touch her, and tell my mind to shut up. It's not doing me or anyone else any favours. Pacing her driveway, I wonder how early is too early. I should have just waited in my car and avoided this awkward situation and given her the time to finish getting ready. I look at my watch. Only a minute has passed since I last looked at it.

"Are you going to come inside or what?" Cecilia calls out. I turn and find her standing in the doorway, looking like a rock goddess.

Combat boots; a distressed, black denim skirt with enough holes to be provocative without being indecent; a lacy, red see-through crop top showcasing her beautiful tits in a red bra; and a black leather jacket. You would think the red shirt and hair would clash, but not at all. Her hair falls down her back, cascading in waves, and I am offered the view of her unguarded face. She doesn't have her glasses on yet. Just looking at her has me hardening in my jeans.

"Well?" she asks again. "I know you are there, Maverick. I heard your car pull up five minutes ago. You can come in."

"C—I—wow," I blurt out, my brain empty due to all the blood rushing south.

"Speechless, I like it!" Cecilia chuckles. "I must have dressed right then!"

Like a dog on a leash, I follow her into her house and cross my arms in an effort to refrain from reaching out and grabbing her.

"You look amazing," I offer, having somewhat regained brain power.

"Thanks. I'd say the same, but I don't think you'd believe me."

I let out a sputtering laugh and reel it in when I realise that might be the wrong reaction, but she throws me a grin. "Dark humour. I love it," I reply.

"So, what are we doing today?" Cecilia asks tentatively.

"Getting to know each other," I reply, knowing it's not exactly the answer she was hoping for. "I know I am early, but are you ready to go?"

"Yeah, let me grab my bag."

She scoops up a small handbag, puts on her sunglasses, and extends her cane. I lead her out to my car, relishing in the feel of having her hand wrapped around my arm. I will never get tired of having her skin on mine.

As I start my car, the radio starts playing "Seen" by Fly By, and I chuckle at the irony of it.

"Please turn it up," Cecilia asks, and I oblige and even sing along, careful to keep my voice lower so she cannot recognise it—not that I am any more than back-up vocals anyway. I'm officially one of those artists who sings along to their own songs in the car.

It feels weirdly right singing with Cecilia as we trade off singing the verses. I have never felt this way with anyone, other than my brothers. When "Seen" ends, we continue singing along to every song that comes on the radio. Cecilia wasn't lying when she said she had a range in her music tastes.

Her voice is just as sweet when she sings, powerful enough to hit some high notes.

I pull into the carpark of Smash It! and let out a hesitant breath. This is a really weird first date location, to be honest, but it's quirky and I have been wanting to try this place out for months.

Grabbing my bag, I help Cecilia out of the car and we walk inside, still buzzing from our rock concert in the car.

"Welcome to Smash It! I'm Jamie. How are you today?" a young man asks as we enter the reception area. I made several requests when I booked out the whole venue: staff are not to act like I am famous, they're to act like the venue is still open to the general public, and in return, they get a large payday and some merch.

Cecilia turns to me, shock evident on her face. "You brought me to Smash It!" she squeals. "This is that rage room where you can break stuff, right?"

"Uh—" I hesitate. "Is that okay?"

"Oh, Maverick! It's more than okay! I have been wanting to come here for ages. My parents always said it would be too dangerous for me."

"No need to worry about that here," Jamie answers for me. "We are more than able to keep everything safe for you in your time here today."

Cecilia's face brightens with the most amazing smile, and I know that for as long as she lets me be in her life, putting that smile on her face will be the only goal I have.

The team at Smash It! do a great job explaining the equipment, how it works, and making adjustments to be inclusive of Cecilia's vison impairment.

"Okay, so we are going to start off in the plate room today!" Jamie informs us, leading us into the prep area. "The goal is to make as much noise as possible. You will each get fifteen plates to smash by throwing them against the floor or wall. Please put on these protective overalls and glasses to prevent you from receiving any injuries from rogue flying items."

Jamie directs us to their locker rooms, and I notice a female staff member announcing herself to Cecilia and offering her assistance to get her stuff stored. Cecilia is almost jumping out of her skin when we emerge from the locker rooms. I grin from her infectious excitement. The overalls are made out of a scratchy cotton, and I have worn something similar playing paintball with my brothers. They are unflattering and no one can look good in them—except for Cecilia. She still looks gorgeous, bundled up in the baggy outfit, blacked out goggles covering half of her face. (Yes, I brought spray painted goggles so that the lights wouldn't affect her while she couldn't wear her glasses.) I just want to kiss her.

We are led into the plate room, and I help position Cecilia so she's facing the throw zone.

"You can go first, baby," I offer.

She picks up her first plate and—with great aim and force—thrusts it forward, causing it to smash into pieces against the far wall.

"I did it!" she squeals in laughter, jumping on the spot.

"Yeah, you did, C!" I exclaim, hugging her from behind. She is practically vibrating in my arms.

We break all our plates, and then go break TVs with a base-ball bat, throw darts at balloons full of paint, and finish by breaking glass bottles by throwing them and smashing them with a baton. There is also a room with old records that you could snap, but in the name of music, we couldn't find it in ourselves to break them.

Cecilia throws the last glass bottle and gushes, "Wow, Maverick! That was amazing!"

"I'm glad you enjoyed it, baby." I sweep her hair behind her ear, leaning down and placing a kiss against her forehead, avoiding the goggles still covering her face.

"Thank you."

"No need to thank me, Cecilia."

"Not for the date. Thank you for treating me like a regular person."

"Wait," I say sarcastically, "you aren't a regular person? Are you an alien?"

She laughs at me, putting that stunning smile on her face again, and I can't resist another second.

"Is it okay if I kiss you?" I ask, unable to resist her, but giving her the option to say no this time and not just attacking her like our first kiss.

Cecilia nods silently, consenting.

My hands move and cup her face, sliding the goggles up and off her head. The room around us fades, my focus solely on Cecilia. Leading down, I press a soft kiss to the corner of her mouth. I pull back, hesitating to kiss her as passionately as I want to. Cecilia's bottom lip sticks out in a pout.

"That's it?" she whines, and I chuckle.

Cecilia's hands twist in my hair, holding me in place and pulling my mouth to hers—crashing them together in a fierce embrace. My arms wrap around her waist, holding her to me. My hands twist into the starchy cotton of her overalls and I lose myself in her mouth. Her fingernails dig into my scalp, pulling on my hair to position my mouth to where she wants it. My left hand dips to palm her ass, and she moans into my mouth. Cecilia leans into my body, and I feel my cock harden in my jeans. Her hands cup my face, tracing over my beard before falling to my chest, palms spread against my chest, her hands gripping the material of my overalls as if she hates it and wants it gone. I know the feeling. I squeeze her ass again, keeping her pressed up against me, letting her feel the erection. She's the only one who's made me hard since I met her.

"Ahem." Someone clears their throat, reminding me that we are in the middle of Smash It! and all the staff members are watching us.

"Fuck." I chuckle, placing another small peck on her lips before I pull back, putting some space between us but still holding onto her. "We should probably get out of here, C. There is more to this date, and we are probably due at the next part now."

I look down at her face, lips swollen, a pink blush marking her cheeks, panting to catch her breath. All I want to do right now is press her up against the closest surface and fuck her until she can't remember her own name. I groan, taking my hands from her back to adjust myself in my jeans. After three weeks of jerking off to thoughts of her, you would think I would be immune to this. She has me in more knots than a fucking macramé.

"There's more?" she asks, still breathless. "This date is already more than enough, Maverick."

"There will always be more, C."

We separate as we get out of the overalls, and before she finishes, I rush over to meet Jamie back out in the lobby.

"Hey, she doesn't know who I am," I whisper to him, "so any selfies that go online can't have her in them." He nods and the staff quickly have their turns meeting me and taking a photo with me. Thankfully, Cecilia is taking her time. Guilt twists me at keeping all these secrets from her. I hope she will understand when she finds out.

I hand my bag over to Jamie, pulling out signed T-shirts, CDs, photographs, and other merch for the staff to share amongst themselves.

"There is one of everything for everyone," I tell him.

"One of what?" Cecilia asks, emerging from the locker room and walking up next to me.

"How did you know where I was?" I ask, changing the subject and wrapping my arm around her, enjoying the feel of her sinking into me.

"Jessie pointed me in the right direction." She frowns. "That, and your voice."

"I like the sound of you following my voice," I breathe into her ear, grinning as I feel a shiver wrack her body. "You ready to go?" I ask her, receiving a silent nod in return.

Twelve - Cecilia

MAVERICK SINGS along to Def Leppard on the radio as he drives us to the next stage of our date. This man is a serious conundrum. How is it that he can be so imperfectly perfect? I told myself that I wouldn't get swept up in him, wouldn't fall for his tricks again. Yet here I am, sitting here in awe of him.

Every time he treats me like a person and not just my disability, I want to kiss him—and what a kisser he is. Each kiss we have shared has been so different. Our kiss earlier was so explosive, I wanted nothing more than to fall into him, to see where that kiss could lead to. When we were alerted we were not alone, I was amazed—and slightly embarrassed—that Maverick would kiss me like *that* in public. Every time our lips touch, I get swept up in him, and even with my conflicted feelings, I cannot bring myself to regret kissing him. It feels too perfect—too right—to regret.

I was hesitant about coming out on this date today. I told myself I forgave him, but I'm not sure if it is something that I can truly let pass. I have been burned so many times by people who I believed were my friend, only to find out that they were trying to make themselves look better by being nice to "that blind girl."

To someone who doesn't have my crap-ton of baggage, Maverick ghosting on them for a few weeks might not be that big a deal. But to me, it was another announcement that something is wrong with me, that I'm not good enough for someone like Maverick to pursue and—maybe—eventually love. Three weeks of pain and hurt didn't go away overnight because he said sorry, and I was hesitant to give him another chance to hurt me again. Yet here I am, giving him his chance.

"We're here," Maverick singsongs while exiting the car. He has my door open before I can orientate myself.

"Where is *here*, exactly?" I ask.

"Ristorante del Treno Pazzo," he replies, pronouncing each word perfectly. The Crazy Train Restaurant. It is a fancy Italian restaurant that has been open for a few years on the east side of the city. They have amazing reviews and are stupid expensive.

"Wow," I reply, not having any other words.

He leads me up several steps before reaching around me to hold the front door open for us.

"Good afternoon, how may I help you today?" A chirpy feminine voice announces as we enter the lobby.

"Reservation for Maverick." I jump in surprise at Maverick's voice so close to my ear, his breath fanning across my head.

"Of course. This way," the hostess replies, and Maverick leads me through the restaurant. He pulls out my chair and helps me sit, being chivalrous.

If I am not careful, I am going to fall in love with this man. He is already starting to ruin all men for me.

The hostess hands me a menu, and before I can tell her that I can't read it, I feel little dots under my fingers.

"I'll send your waiter over for you," the hostess states, walking away from the table.

I run my fingertips over the paper. This is a braille menu. Tears sting the back of my eyes. I have never felt so accepted in my whole life, and to be granted something so small as being able to read by myself has me on the verge of being a blubbering mess.

"Are you okay?" Maverick asks, panic in his voice.

"Y-yeah." I clear my throat and then immediately worry about how unattractive that sound was. "I'm fine."

"You can tell me, you know. Do you want to go somewhere else?"

"It's not that—it's just so rare that restaurants are this accommodating," I say, gesturing to the menu in my hands.

"How is it normally?" Maverick asks, voice full of compassion.

"Servers generally ignore me, speaking only to whoever I am with. I have spoken to you before about some of my struggles, but today has been a little bit overwhelming. I have been treated like a person every time I am in your presence. And unfortunately, it is not something I am used to."

"I'm sorry, C. No one should be made to feel like that."

"Sadly, it is what is normal for me, and for the majority of the disabled population. But with people like you, and places like this restaurant, the world will start changing, and eventually this will be the norm." I smile at him. "Is the décor as amazing as they say?" I ask to change the subject.

"It is pretty great." I hear the smile in his voice.

"Explain it to me, please?"

"When we entered the restaurant, the hostess stand looks like an old ticket booth. It's a big wooden bench and window where people used to buy their tickets—before everything went digital, that is. Then each chair is an old train seat. They are all mismatched; different designs and colours litter every chair. Some are abstract, some are just plain lines or polka dots. The tables are screen printed to look like train tracks, and the walls are covered in photos of old trains or old train parts."

"Are you serious?" I ask, baffled. Surely he just made that all up.

"C, I wouldn't lie to you. When they say crazy train—they mean it."

I laugh, swept up in the energy that this man exudes.

We both take our time perusing the menu, discussing the options and our preferences.

"Hi, folks, Welcome to Ristorante del Treno Pazzo. My name is Paul, and I will be looking after you for the rest of the evening. Are you ready to order?" I hear a server ask.

"Yes. Cecilia?" Maverick asks, indicating that I should order first.

"Can I have the chicken lasagne?" I ask Paul. It snagged my notice, as lasagne is normally made with beef, and it seems strange to me. So strange that I need to try it out.

"Of course. Sir?"

"I will have the pescatori, please." Again with the perfect Italian pronunciation. Maverick is not making it easy to not swoon for him.

Paul takes our menus and our drink order before leaving us alone.

"Why is it so quiet?" I ask, realising for the first time that I cannot hear anyone else in the restaurant.

"Uh—we are in a private room." Maverick answers, sounding unsure if that was the right answer. Strange, but I decide it's not worth pushing.

I twist my fingers in my lap, suddenly nervous.

"So, this got awkward fast," I say.

"You are nothing if not direct, Cecilia."

"Life is short; it's better to be direct. And I can't read body language the same as everyone else. So sometimes I have to prompt others along."

"How do you want to prompt me along?" he asks, lowering his voice, husky and seductive. This man.

"Want to play twenty questions?" I ask, flustered. I'm not sure why that was the first thing that came to mind.

"Twenty questions?" he repeats, puzzled.

"Sorry, it's the first thing that came to my head. We don't have to…" I trail off.

"No, it's okay. You just caught me by surprise. I haven't played that game in a while. Do you mean the object-guessing one? Or just asking each other twenty random questions?"

"The second one." I blush.

"Any rules or restrictions as to what we can ask?"

"No." I pause to think. "But we have the right to refuse to answer a question. This is only our first date."

"Second date," he corrects me.

"Second date? I don't think the other one counts. For all you know, I had a concussion."

"I think it counts. You were very lucid. We got to know each other, shared a meal and a kiss...that's the definition of a date."

"Okay, fine," I relent, blushing. "It's our second date, and second date rules apply."

"What are the second date rules, exactly?"

"You know."

"No, I don't. I haven't had a second date in a while," he replies nervously.

"Really?" I exclaim.

"Not for lack of trying, but no. It's been a while since I had anything serious," he tacks on under his breath, not meaning for me to hear.

"What's wrong with you?" I ask bluntly.

"What?"

"Sorry, that came out wrong. I just mean, why don't they want to keep dating you? You are this amazing, sweet, sensitive, funny guy. I don't understand why they would pass you up."

"I don't know. Maybe you just see more to me than everyone else did."

"How do you mean?" There's another side to Maverick? I already want to know him, but now I crave it.

"Not tonight, C. Next question."

My heart deflates. I was on the tip of an iceberg with him, and he pushed me back down again.

"How old were you when you got your first kiss?" I ask.

"Fourteen. You?"

"Is that your question?"

"Yes."

"I was twenty."

"How old are you now?" he asks.

"Ah! Not your turn, and don't you know to never ask a woman her age? Hmm. What is your favourite colour?" I ask.

"Purple. What's your guilty pleasure?"

"Watching trivia or game TV shows."

"Really?" Maverick asks.

"Yep, I can't get enough of them. I love playing along and seeing if I beat the contestants."

"Would you ever go on one of them?"

"Hey," I exclaim, "that would be your third question in a row. My turn. You said before that you love romance things. Does anyone else know that about you?"

He mentioned it on our apparent first date, and it has been swirling around in my head. The stickers, the verging on stalking—I guess, in a way, it would be classified as romantic.

"Only my family. No one else. I kinda have a reputation to keep up."

"Maybe that's why none of those girls stuck around—they believe the reputation to be the real you."

"Are you complaining that other women left me single?"

"No!" I yell before I can stop myself, blushing. "Shit, sorry. No, I—uh—guess not?" My voice rises, turning my statement into a question, and he chuckles.

"Okay, so back to my earlier question: Would you go onto a game show?"

"I guess it would depend on the show and the host," I answer honestly, glad to move on from my dramatic outburst. "If I were treated just like a sighted contestant, yes. But if I was the new poster child for blindness so sighted people can gawk at me because I amazingly accomplish simple tasks—then no."

"I can understand that."

"What colour are your eyes?" It's an irrelevant question for me to ask, really. I don't know what colours look like to other people, although I have always been curious, but it's another thing about him that I just need to know.

"They are hazel. Have you ever thought about being an advocate for blind or disabled people? Being the voice that tells all the inconsiderate bastards what they are doing wrong?"

"Yes, I have, but why me? Why do I have to be the person who stands up for us? Why can't sighted people just do the right thing? Why can't they just educate themselves? It shouldn't be up to a vision impaired person to teach someone common curtesy. Apart from our disability, we are the same and should be treated as such."

"I am sorry, Cecilia, I don't mean to upset you."

"It's okay, it's a valid question. It's just a touchy subject for me. Obviously." I laugh.

Paul arrives with our food and drinks, distracting me with the savoury scents of béchamel sauce and cheese.

"I think it is your turn to ask a question," Maverick says once Paul leaves.

"Have you ever been to Europe?"

"Yes, I have been to the UK and to several countries in Europe in the last few years," he replies.

"Where was your favourite?" I ask as I place a bite of my lasagne in my mouth. I moan around my fork, shamelessly intoxicated by the amazing taste. "Maverick?" I prompt when he hasn't responded, "What's wrong?"

"Wha—? Nothing. Sorry, just got distracted there. What did you ask me?"

"Where in Europe is your favourite?" I moan again as I swallow another delicious bite of my dinner.

"Fuck, you need to stop that," he growls.

"Stop what?" I ask, confused. I'm only asking him questions as part of our game.

"The moaning. It's too much."

"Oh, um—sorry?"

"You have no idea how sexy you are, do you?"

"Is that your question?" I ask, trying to delay answering.

"If that will get you to answer, then yes, it is my question."

"I guess I have never thought of myself as sexy, no. Taylor tells me I am beautiful. But I wouldn't know how I compare to everyone else, and Taylor has to be nice to me since she is my sister."

"No guys ever told you how bewitching you are?"

"It's not like guys have been lining up to take me out."

"Well, let me tell you, on behalf of all the stupid men in the world: you are amazingly, devastatingly beautiful, inside and out. It's not just your looks—which, trust me, are stunning, but it's you as a whole."

I sit there, stunned. Speechless. No idea how to respond to that. I would like to throw myself at him like a swooning damsel from a romance movie, but I can't move. No one's ever said such powerful, emotive, honest words to me before. And I can tell he is being honest. There is no way the passion in his voice could have been faked.

"Th-thank you," I stammer out.

"You are welcome, Cecilia. I will tell you every day until it sinks in just how incredible you are."

"Wow."

"So you didn't answer me earlier, how old are you?"

"Um, twenty."

"So who was your first kiss?"

"You."

"Whoa," Maverick replies, shocked. "I am honoured."

I blush as we continue eating, asking each other questions and opening up to each other. I was afraid before, but now I am certain: I am falling for this man.

Thirteen - Maverick

"THANK YOU FOR TODAY, MAVERICK," Cecilia says sweetly, smiling up at me as we stand on her porch.

Having finished our lunch and lingering over an amazing dessert platter—cannoli, tiramisu, panna cotta, and gelato—I reluctantly drove her home, wishing I could do anything to extend our time together.

"I had a great time too, Cecilia." I trail my calloused fingertips down her soft cheek, needing to touch her. A need to do more than just touch her jolts through me. Using my other hand, I palm my cock in my jeans, rearranging it to be more comfortable and silently commanding it to behave while I tilt her head up, keeping my finger hooked under her chin. "Is this okay?" I breathe against her mouth, my voice husky with my desire.

Cecilia's eyes close and she leans into me, brushing her lips against mine, a feeling I will remember forever. I'm amazed at her initiating our kiss, reaffirming for me that she really does want this too. I kiss her back, turning her sweet caress into something deeper, more primal as my need for her takes over my mind. My tongue plays with the seam of her mouth, asking for entrance. Air whooshes out of me as Cecilia's tongue softly caresses mine. The inner caveman in me wants to throw her over my shoulder and show the world she is mine, to claim her and keep her forever.

Cecilia's soft hands startle me as she trails her fingertips up the sides of my neck, clasping at the back of my neck and holding me to her. She steps into me, our bodies now flush against each other, the evidence of what she does to me sticking into her stomach.

"Do you want to come inside?" Cecilia asks breathlessly, pulling back only to trail kisses down my cheek, mapping my jawline with the tip of her tongue. "My sister is at work."

"Yes." I know I should take things slower with her, but this woman has ensnared me. I would do anything for her—anything she wants or needs, I would give to her the second she asks.

I reluctantly step back, allowing Cecilia space to turn around and open the door. The moment her back is to me, I press into her, holding her waist with my hands and trailing my nose down the curve of her neck. My Cecilia is worth so much more to me than another one-night stand, and I am not going to treat her like one. Once the door is open, she leads me through to her living room again, easing out of my arms to sit on her couch.

Sitting next to her, I wrap my arm around her shoulders and pull her into me, meeting her mouth in another kiss. Her lips make demands mine are eager to meet. Cecilia is quickly ruining me for all other women, tempting me with soft caresses and sweet kisses. Without breaking our kiss, Cecilia manages to twist in her seat, throwing her leg over my lap and straddling me.

"Wha're you doin'?" I pant, slurring my words in her mouth.

"Need to be closer," she whispers, just as breathless as me. A sense of pride fills me, knowing I did that to her.

My hands fall to her hips, holding her steady as she continues to possess my mouth. Cecilia opens her legs further, pressing her centre against my aching cock. We moan as we make contact, I grab her ass and grind her against me, giving into the tempting seductress Cecilia is.

"Let me make you feel good?" I ask, nibbling on her earlobe.

"Mhm, yes, Maverick—"

I trail my lips down her neck, skimming over her collarbone. Cecilia takes off her leather jacket and I raise my hands to the hem of her crop top, brushing against her waist.

"We stop whenever you want to. Let me know if you want me to do something or stop, okay? I don't want you feeling uncomfortable."

"Don't stop, please, Maverick. I need…" She trails off in a moan as my jean-covered cock thrusts against her panties. Skirts really are a man's best friend. I lift her top, needing more contact with her, causing her to shift back and show me that creamy skin, her vibrant red hair curling over her shoulders and down her back. The red bra she wears looks amazing on her, but it will look even better on the floor. I reach around and release those beautiful boobs, freeing them to sway in front of my face. My lips move, kissing her collarbone again and moving further down as I cup her breasts. My thumbs skim over her pink nipples, puckering them. My mouth waters with need to taste her.

I flick my tongue over her nipple, causing Cecilia to arch her back into me. I explore her, switching between her nipples and worshiping her body as she deserves. Cecilia shifts her hips against me, grinding against my dick. The thought of her using me for her pleasure has me leaking precum in my briefs.

"More, Mav," she pleads, and I am not strong enough to tell her no.

"I won't fuck you." I groan at the thought of being inside her tight, wet heat. A frown creases her brow and I explain, "You deserve more than a rough fuck on the couch on our second date." Her whimper almost has me changing my mind, but I can make her feel good without needing to fuck her.

I lift her off my lap and deposit her back onto the couch, ignoring her protests as I stand and sink to my knees on the floor. She is beauty personified: crazy, wild hair cascading over her shoulders and the couch; topless, her breasts drawing my eye with her laboured breaths. Her denim mini skirt has ridden up, giving me a peek at her red panties—which match the discarded bra—and combat boots.

"One day, I want to fuck you with just these boots on," I say gruffly, unlacing her boots, removing them, and not caring where they went once they were off her amazing legs. Cecilia quivers as I trail soft kisses up the insides of her legs, stopping at her knees. I look up at her. "Is this okay?" I ask, needing her consent before I continue.

"Uh-huh." She nods, breathless. Another burst of pride fills me, knowing that I make her feel like this.

"I am sorry, I don't have a dental dam here. I've been cleared recently, but if you prefer, I can just use my hands."

"N-no. I trust you, Maverick. I don't have anything either, I've —ah—never done anything like this before. Please touch me. I need to feel you touch me." Cecilia whimpers, causing my cock to harden in my pants. I want nothing more than to taste my girl on my tongue. I would have used protection or done something different to get her off if she insisted, but knowing I am about to taste her—and be the first to—has my mind fogging up. Nothing else exists but me, my girl, and her pleasure. I continue up her creamy pale thighs, my fingers reaching ahead and pulling her ass forward on the seat.

My fingers tease her hips, playing with the strings of her panties, hooking in, and dragging them down—but not removing them yet. I inch forward, hypnotized by the sight of her panty-clad pussy, a damp spot starting to bloom, darkening the fabric and heightening my desire. I place my face against Cecilia's core and inhale her sweet scent. Unable to hold back any longer, I shove her panties down and place a kiss at the centre of my Cecilia, raising my hands slowly back up her legs, wrapping around her ass to hold her to me.

Nothing could compare to Cecilia. The way she moans, wriggles against my face, her taste. I am in heaven. I lick a line up her lips, pausing to suck and flick my tongue against her clit.

"Please…Maverick…" Cecilia whimpers, clearly needing more.

I move my tongue back down to her entrance, circling her hole and teasing her, lapping at her wetness. I could do this forever. I trail my eyes up her body, pride sweeping through me at the look of bliss and pleading on her face. I part her lips and dart my tongue inside, softly fucking her with my tongue. I raise my left hand from her ass to her tits, squeezing the bountiful handfuls softly before pinching her nipples, alternating to give her the most pleasure.

"Yes, yes, yes," Cecilia chants, lost in the moment.

I switch between plunging my tongue into her depths and rising back to flick and suck on her clit. Her body shakes as I push her to the edge before pulling back, letting her settle before doing it all over again. My cock leaks in my jeans, sad for the lack of involvement—but this is about Cecilia. Her pleasure is enough for me.

"More, Maverick, please," Cecilia whines, and I feel the need rising in her again. My left hand is still playing with her tits, so I slowly move my right hand from palming that gorgeous ass to her hip. She shifts, knowing my game and silently asking me to move faster. I trail my fingertips over her hip bone, loving the way her skin rises in goosebumps.

My fingers brush against her delicate flesh, and Cecilia wiggles, trying to get my fingers lower, where she wants them. She whimpers at the loss as I pull my face back and look down at my hands against her. Her thighs are red from my beard, her lips glistening, dripping her desire that's just asking to be played with. I could do this all day—playing with her, bringing her close but denying her to climax.

"Maverick—" Cecilia moans.

I am overwhelmed with the trust Cecilia has placed in me to be her first, with her being open to me like this. "Yes, baby?" I ask sweetly.

"Maverick, I—I need—"

"What do you need, Cecilia?"

"Anything—everything—"

"You want to cum? You want to find your release with my tongue against this sweet pussy?"

"Y-yesssssss," she hisses out as I twist her nipple, more wetness pooling against my fingers.

"Okay, baby." I lean in, my fingers moving out of my way as I lick from the underside of her pussy to her clit, lapping up the juices that are rightly mine. Cecilia is quickly becoming the best thing I have ever tasted, better than any of my favourite foods.

When I reach her clit again, I suckle and tease it gently with the flat of my tongue and bring my fingers back to her entrance. I slowly ease one finger into her—so tight and innocent—running my callused fingers against her rough walls, drawing more moans from her. I press into her front wall, trailing until I find her G-spot sitting there calmly, waiting to be caressed too. I press against it, and Cecilia moans and wiggles more. I keep it up, sucking and flicking her clit, pushing my finger in and out of her. I don't want to hurt her, so I keep it to one finger. I wiggle my finger and tongue in sync, pushing her higher and higher. Cecilia's hands drop and twist into my hair, holding my face against her pussy as she reaches her climax. I keep licking as she climaxes, cleaning up the mess I made and tasting each sweet drop she grants me. As she starts to come down from her high, I pull back, licking my lips to savour her on me.

"Whoa," she sighs breathlessly.

Chuckling, I rise to my feet and sit back on the couch next to her. Drawing her into my arms, I cuddle into her, dropping my head to her lips and kissing her softly before letting her snuggle into my neck. It should probably feel weird to be fully clothed and holding Cecilia while she is naked—all except her skirt, which is still bunched around her waist—but it's not.

"Okay, time to get you cleaned up and dressed. I wouldn't want you catching a cold," I murmur into her hair, dropping a kiss on top of her head.

Cecilia leans back, pulls her face out from my neck, and blesses me with a huge smile, knocking the breath out of me.

Fourteen - Cecilia

"WHAT ABOUT YOU?" I ask quietly. I have never felt anything like what Maverick just made me feel, and I want to repay the favour.

"Today wasn't about me, love. I am happy you are happy; that's all that matters," Maverick replies, his voice stern to brook no arguments. He really believes that I will let him go without returning his advances?

"Will you help me shower?" I ask demurely. "Normally Tay would help me." A complete lie—I haven't needed help in the bathroom since I was five. Like the rest of our house, I have learned where my products are—kept in the same space and order for my ease of use—and I am able to shower or bathe without assistance. Maverick doesn't need to know that yet, though.

"Um—sure, okay." He hesitates, and I realise this time, I will need to take the initiative.

I rise from the couch, pulling my skirt completely off me as I stand. "Will you please pass me my other clothes? I don't want to leave them around for Taylor to find later."

"Of course." I hear rustling as he collects all my clothes and boots. "I'll carry them. Do you want them in your room?"

"Yeah, there is a laundry basket next to the wardrobe door, and there will be space in my shoe rack for the boots." I quickly find clean shorts, panties, and a T-shirt to wear before we are both ready to head to the bathroom down the hall.

My hands shake as nerves fill me. Why am I nervous? It's not like he hasn't already seen me naked—hell, I am *still* naked. But how will he feel about me touching him?

I have never done anything remotely sexual. Taylor has told me a lot about her encounters, teaching me what to expect. I have played around with myself before, but nothing could compare to the way Maverick made me feel.

The sound of the bathroom door opening causes my heartbeat to pick up. Maverick moves into the room, draws back the shower curtain, and starts the shower.

"Do you just need me to help you get inside?" he asks nervously. The sound of his nerves puts mine at ease. This is something new for him too. Maybe not in the same way, but I can do this.

"I need you to come in with me."

"Cecilia, I don't know if that is a good idea. Surely Taylor doesn't always shower *with* you."

"But I need your help," I say as innocently as possible while restraining a grin. I can practically feel his shields dropping. "Please come shower with me, Maverick?"

"Okay," he sighs, and I'm not going to take it personally that he sounds like he doesn't want to shower with me. "Let me get you in, and I will join you."

Maverick holds onto my biceps, ensuring I have steady footing as he deposits me under the warm water. My arms tingle where he touches me, and I feel myself pout as he pulls back.

He chuckles at my protests. "I just have to take my clothes off."

I hear Maverick take off his shoes. Anticipation courses through me as he undoes his belt, the zipper of his jeans pulling down. A shiver runs up my spine at the mere thought of this man being naked so close to me. He steps into the shower, touching my arm gently to alert me to his location.

"Okay, you got me here. What do you need my help with first?"

"Can you wash my back?" I ask, turning around to give him access.

Maverick steps into me, reaching around to grab my loofah and cover it in my body wash. With the loofah in one hand, he trails his free fingertips down my spine. I arch my back, pushing my ass back toward him. He chuckles as he manoeuvres his body so I don't touch him, unfortunately. He runs his hands over my back, washing and caressing me, gently rubbing the loofah down my arms.

Placing his hands on my shoulders, he turns me around, trailing his fingers across my collarbone. His other hand raises to run the loofa over my stomach. Seizing the opportunity while his guard is down, I twist my hand between us, placing it directly on top of his dick—or should I say, his underwear.

"Why are you wearing underwear in the shower?" I ask, leaving my hand on the soaked material clinging to every inch of him—and it's a lot of inches.

"I, uh…didn't think you'd be comfortable with me being naked."

"Why not?" I mean, I did ask him to get into the shower with me.

"Well, I didn't want to force myself on you."

I sigh. "How are you real?"

"I don't know how to answer that." He laughs. "Cecilia?"

"Hmm?"

"You are still touching my cock…"

"You noticed that, huh?"

"Kinda hard not to, babe."

"Mm, is that you telling me no?"

"No."

"So that's a yes, then."

"Mmhmm," he groans, and I follow his voice, leaning in and placing a kiss on the side of his neck before trailing more kisses down and over his collarbone, kissing any skin my lips can reach.

I slip my hand inside his underpants and brush my fingertips against his rigid length, teasing him lightly before moving my hand to the waistband and starting to inch them down. I keep my head buried in his neck, sneaking my tongue out to lick a line up his throat—collecting rivulets of water that have stuck to him. He helps me remove his briefs, and the sound of his cock whacking against his lower stomach as it's released sends a wave of desire through me. I can't help but think about Maverick bending me over, taking me from behind as I lean down to pick up the dropped soap. Or having my legs wrapped around his waist as my back presses into the cold tiles as he pounds up into me.

As much as I want him inside me, he already said no to that tonight, and I won't push him on that.

Bringing myself out of my lusty thoughts, I manage to keep my attention on him. My hand shakes as I wrap my fist around his cock, feeling his fast pulse against my palm. Maverick moans as I squeeze him lightly. I use the fluidity of the water to slowly move my hand up and down his cock, caressing his soft skin. I press my thumb into the underside of his crown, knowing it is usually a sensitive spot, before swiping up over his slit, collecting his precum. I want nothing more than to bring my thumb to my mouth and taste him—like he tasted me—but the water washes his precum away before I get the chance. Maybe doing this in the shower wasn't the best idea after all.

"Kiss me," I whisper. Maverick crashes his mouth to mine mere seconds after the words leave my lips.

His tongue penetrates my mouth, plunging in and tangling with mine, reminding me of what that mouth did to me on the couch. I keep my hand on his dick, becoming more confident stroking and pulling on him, pushing him to find his release. My free hand leans against his chest, and I tentatively run my thumb over his nipple. Maverick lets out a groan, encouraging me to touch him more. I flick, pinch, and twist his nipples as he moans into my mouth, and he begins to thrust into my fist, losing control as his cock hardens even more inside my hand.

"Cecilia—" He says my name like a prayer, somehow both a question and an answer. "Cecilia—"

"Maverick," I say softly as he groans and releases his cum all over my hand and stomach.

He brings his mouth softly to mine, our kiss full of emotions I can't even begin to explain, before pulling back and washing his cum off me.

"Whoa."

"What?" I ask, confused.

"I haven't cum that quick and hard since I was a teenager." He chuckles, sounding sheepish.

"Is that a bad thing?" I ask, butterflies in my stomach. I worry my inexperience is showing.

"Other than looking like a two-pump chump, I guess not," he says self-consciously.

"Well, you were worked up after our adventure on the couch. It makes sense, honestly," I reassure him.

Maverick's laugh bounces off the bathroom tiles, wrapping around me. I wish it could hold onto me forever, warming my insides, reminding me of this moment.

"Was it your plan to seduce me the whole time?" he asks.

"Maaaybe," I reply, twisting out of his arms to turn the shower off.

"Come on, let's get you dry and into some comfy clothes," Maverick says, amused with me.

He gently helps me out of the shower, towelling me off in an almost-reverent manner. I dress myself in my clean shorts and shirt as he pulls on his earlier clothes.

"So, I should probably get going…" Maverick says as we re-enter the living room.

"Oh." My heart deflates. I realise I was hoping I could introduce him to Taylor. "Okay."

"I'm sorry, babe, but I have to go to my folks' place early tomorrow morning."

"I understand. I am just sad our time together is ending." I lead him toward the front door, opening it for him to leave.

"No, C, it's just beginning." He places a soft kiss on the tip of my nose, on both of my cheeks, my forehead, and finally— finally—on my lips. "I'll see you soon, baby."

I close the door after I hear his car start. I check my watch, realising it is four in the afternoon and we've spent six hours together. With no plans for the rest of the day, I decide to lie down in bed with my newest audiobook and just relax after an amazing day.

I must've fallen asleep, as I awaken to the sound of Taylor knocking on my door.

"Cecilia…do you want to come out here and explain why there is a pair of men's underpants on the shower floor? Or are you too *busy?*" The insinuation is heavy in her voice.

Shit. So not the way I wanted Taylor to find out.

Fifteen - Maverick

THE LAST FOUR weeks of dating Cecilia have been heavenly. We have gone on almost eight dates—each one more and more amazing than the last. We have managed to go out most days we share a class together and on Saturdays. Narrowly missing Taylor every time has become a challenge, and I think Cecilia is starting to get suspicious of me.

We have had some amazing dates together—picnics on the beach, a private pottery lesson, an afternoon listening to music and comparing our tastes, volunteering for playtime at the local pet shelter and getting kitten and puppy cuddles, and an audio descriptive tour at a museum. I want to do everything with her.

There is no longer any doubt in my mind that I am in love with Cecilia. There's only the small issue that she still doesn't know that I'm a member of her favourite band. This has gone on for so long now, I have no idea how to tell her without losing her.

She is the first person outside of my family to whom I have showed my true self, and losing her is too painful to even think about. Is there anyway—anyway at all—that I can get every-thing I have ever wanted?

We haven't gone any further than third base. I have been nervous to take that step. As a man who has been with more women than I can remember, I want our time together to be special, memorable. I cannot remember the last time I was with a virgin, and I don't want it to be cramped in a back seat or rushed so I can leave before her sister gets home. I thought about bringing her back to my place for the night, but haven't broached the subject yet. It would be hard to have her in my space with my lie still between us.

It has been hard to not give into my desires. With four weeks of heated kisses and the occasional grope, turning Cecilia down—without hurting her feelings—has become more and more complex.

"Mav, man, you in there?" Joel's voice brings me out of my thoughts.

Blinking a few times, I return to the present, in a meeting with our manager, Mitch. "Fuck, sorry guys. What were we talking about?"

"We were just confirming information about the next tour," Mitch recaps for me. "As you all know, the tour kicks off on the fifteenth of February here in the Gold Coast and Brisbane. Like your last tour, you will be doing two to three concerts at each location every week. Across Australia, we have eight cities and twenty-three shows in six weeks. You have a two-week break before we fly to America, touring fifty-six different cities from April to the end of October before continuing on to Canada. You will have a break from December to January, then we will pick back up for the European and Asian leg of the tour, but we are still confirming the dates and locations." This is mostly information that we already know, but Mitch is finalising the details of our schedule. "Reckless Tunez has finalised negotiations for your opening act, and Afterglow will be joining you."

"What?" Joel says.

"Afterglow is managed by Reckless, and as they are funding the tour, the label gets the say. They want to promote your new album and get Afterglow in on your popularity," Mitch explains.

"But Afterglow are country—and they're self-absorbed dicks!" Joel protests. "That's just not going to work!"

"Have you even met them?" Ethan asks.

"That's irrelevant!" Joel states. I take in my brothers' faces and can sense we are all thinking the same thing. Joel is opposing this too much—something has clearly happened between him and someone in Afterglow.

"Too bad, Joel, what the label says, goes." Mitch placates Joel before turning back to the rest of us, cutting off my thoughts. "We will finalise everything for the new album at our next meeting, but so far all the demos sound great and Reckless are happy with them on the new album."

"Good." I exhale, ready to be out of here. "Are we done?"

"Mav's eager to go, as he has a hot date," Ethan stage-whispers to Mitch.

"Is that who the stickers were for?" Mitch asks me.

"Stickers?" my brother's chorus.

"Thanks for that, Mitch." I sigh reluctantly.

"Well, I don't really know anything about it either. Now you can tell us all at once." Mitch grins. He may be about fifteen years older than me, but he has always fitted in well with our group dynamic. At times it feels like he is an extra brother to care for and mess with.

"Well, you guys know about Cecilia." I nod to my brothers. "I had Mitch send me some stickers for her 'cause she is such a huge fan."

"That's not much to go on," Mitch states.

"She know who you are yet?" Tom asks me.

I never told my family that Cecilia is blind. To me, it is a nonfactor— it doesn't change our relationship or the way I see her. They can find out when it becomes relevant to a conversation or they meet her. Mind you, they may already have suspicions after what I have told them so far.

"No," I growl out. I still don't know how to solve that problem, and I do not need my brothers' input. "I gotta go!" I stand up, wave goodbye to everyone, and make my exit out to my car.

Just one more date. One more, then I will tell her. Just to give me one final happy memory before my world implodes.

Too eager for our date tonight, I came straight here from our meeting with Mitch, and I am half an hour early. Again. Before I can debate waiting in the car or not, Cecilia throws the front door open and waits there, giving me an amused smile.

No point in hiding now. I get out of my car, and once I slam the door closed, Cecilia calls out, "Were you just going to wait out here again?"

"I was thinking about it." I chuckle while walking up the driveway to her. Cecilia has amazing style, and she has pulled together another stunning outfit for today: a long, flowing plaid skirt and a tight black tank top, her favourite pair of combat boots peeking out the bottom.

"You look beautiful!" I say, crassly wolf-whistling as she turns to walk back into her house.

"Thank you. I just have to grab my stuff, then I am good to go," Cecilia replies, picking up her handbag and cane. "Where are we off to tonight?"

"There's a restaurant in town that is having a poetry reading tonight, so I thought we could go there and check it out over some dinner. Thoughts?"

"That sounds beautiful."

We leave the house, and I wait while Cecilia locks the door before escorting her to the passenger side of my car.

"How has your Saturday been?" I ask her while starting the car.

"Oh, it was good. I finished off that report for Finance—how did you do with it?" Cecilia replies.

"I think I did okay with it. Time will tell when we hear back from Professor Jones. I cannot wait for that class to be over, though. This is my last semester of uni before I graduate."

"Mine too."

We spend the rest of the drive discussing the assignment and the topics we decided to make our reports on. I chose budgeting for a mortgage, whereas Cecilia chose to do hers on investments in the music industry. I got lucky finding this woman. I have met a few musicians whose partners couldn't understand the pull of the music, and it ended up driving a wedge in their relationship. Thankfully, I don't think we will have that issue. After tonight, I will tell her. One more night of memories before I potentially ruin this forever.

This is the first date we are going on where we will actually be interacting with the public, and it has me filled with nerves. I shouldn't do this while she doesn't know about my fame, but I am hoping tonight we can be lowkey enough that no one will notice me.

"Alright, you ready for this?" I ask jokingly as I park the car.

"Sure." She grins at me, allowing me to help her out of the car and into the restaurant.

I make eye contact with the hostess and see his eyes widen. Fuck, he's made me straightaway.

"Hi, can we have a table for two, please?" I ask quickly, not giving him time to gush or fill Cecilia in on who I am. I raise my hands in a placating motion, urging him to remain calm.

"S-s-s-sure," he stutters out, and I can't tell if it is because I have overwhelmed him or not.

"Sorry to be a pain, but can it be *away* from the main section?"

"Yes, s-s-sir. Please follow me."

We follow him through a maze of tables before being seated at a small booth in the back corner of the restaurant. I sit with my back to the majority of the restaurant, trying to conceal myself as much as possible.

"Here are your menus. My name is Tony, and I will look after you tonight. Can I get you any drinks to start off with?"

"C?"

"Coke, please," Cecilia replies softly.

"Two Cokes, please, Tony."

"S-sure. I-I'll be right back." Tony rushes off like a bat out of hell, and I know that within minutes, the whole staff will know that I am here.

"I have to go to the bathroom, C. I'll be back in a second, okay?" I say, standing up and brushing a kiss on Cecilia's hand.

"No problem, Maverick." She smiles at me sweetly and I want nothing more than to sit here and talk to her, but I have damage control to do.

I quickly walk through the restaurant toward the bar and find Tony there, filling our drinks and gossiping with his co-workers.

"I swear! Mav is here—why would I lie to you about that? We all know he lives in the city, but I have never seen him around before. He is hotter in person, and man, that voice—" Tony trails off as a petite blonde elbow him, and Tony looks up and spots me. "Shit."

"It's all good." I laugh softly to break the tension. "I'm sorry to ambush you over here, but my date doesn't know I am Mav, okay? I need you to keep it to yourself, please."

"You…are talking to me…" Tony whispers.

"Sure am." Wow, this boy sure is starstruck.

"Me…"

This could take a while. "As I said, I need you to treat me like a normal patron over there, okay?"

"Uh-huh." He nods, noncommittal.

"Alright, good. Thank you." I awkwardly pat the bar twice before pushing off and walking back through the restaurant, keeping my head down to not attract any more unwanted attention.

"Any idea what you feel like?" I ask Cecilia while reclaiming my seat.

"Do they have any wings?"

I check over the menu. "Yep. Buffalo, barbeque, and honey sesame."

"Delicious."

Tony returns with our drinks, looking flustered. "Uh—your drinks. Have you had a chance to decide on mains?" he asks, not stammering this time.

"Yes. Cecilia?"

"I will have the barbeque wings, please. Can I have sour cream on the side?"

"Of course, miss." Tony enters the order into his iPad and turns to me. "And for you, s-sir?"

"I'll have the barbeque wings too. Can you just make it one large serving and we will split it?"

"Okay, no problem, will be along with that shortly." Tony turns on his heel and shuffles away awkwardly.

"Welcome, everyone, to our open poetry night!" A high trill calls through a microphone on the other side of the dining room. "We have a few people signed up to share their work tonight—if you can please put your hands together for Simon!"

The customers all clap as Simon steps onstage and Cecilia and I sit back in our booth, listening to Simon read his poems of love and heartbreak. Tony brings out our food toward the end of Simon's third poem, and the announcer comes back onstage to welcome the next artist.

We pick away at our food, listening to the poems and discussing them in the breaks between. I love how we listen to the same exact poems, but her takes on them are so different, opening my eyes to feel the art the way she feels it. It is one of the best dates we have been on—just being with her, spending time together.

Sixteen - Cecilia

IS it too soon to tell him I love him? It's only been a month—four weeks full of amazing dates, adventures, and getting to know Maverick. I had never put much stock into the whole "soulmates" thing, but I can no longer deny that Maverick is perfect for me. I wasn't expecting to find a man—or anyone, really—who knew me and accepted me this well. He treats me better than even my family does at times.

We're sitting in my driveway after leaving the poetry reading, and I don't want the night to end.

"Do you want to come inside? Taylor is out for the night." I don't care if we just sit there in silence. I just want to be with him.

"I was going to ask you if I could come in." He chuckles.

We head into my house, and he plops on the couch while I fetch us water from the kitchen.

"So what did you think about tonight?" he asks as I sit down next to him. I hand him his bottle of water and his other arm wraps around me, snuggling me into his side.

"I loved it. Thank you. I had never been to a poetry reading like that before. I especially liked the poem using driving as a metaphor for his relationship."

"Good, I enjoyed that one too." Maverick places a kiss to the top of my head, letting the conversation fall away.

If I didn't know better, I would say that Maverick isn't interested in me sexually anymore. We have had a few make out sessions over the last few weeks, but nothing like our first real date together again. There have been a few times I have been desperate for him, but Maverick always finds a way to turn me down—"Taylor will be here soon;" "I need to go to Mum and Dad's." I was certain that he was allowing me to set the pace, but if that's the case, why does he keep turning me down when I press for more?

Testing this, I twist my torso, tilting my face up and seeking out his mouth. He must know what I am after, as a second later he presses his lips to mine, barely brushing against each other. Soft and sweet is not what I am after tonight. I flick my tongue out and lick the seam of his mouth, silently begging for access. Getting bolder, I drop my hand to his crotch, and joy pulses through me at the feel of his hard dick pressing against his zipper. I squeeze gently and I am rewarded with a moan, his mouth falling open and finally granting me access to play with his tongue.

Our kiss becomes more intense, his teeth tugging on my lower lip—his tongue soothing over the sting before plunging back into my mouth. I could kiss him for hours, but tonight I need more than just kissing.

My hand still palming his cock, I drop my lips to his jawline, trailing along and down his neck until I nibble on his earlobe.

"C, what are you doing?" he pants.

"I want you," I whisper as seductively as I can manage in his ear.

"You already have me, baby."

"I do?"

"Yeah, I am yours," he growls softly. Those words shoot a flare of desire through my body, pinging to every single nerve.

"In that case…" Shifting, I hike up my skirt and straddle Maverick's lap. His hands grip my waist to steady me.

"What are you doing?" he asks teasingly.

"I am going to take what's mine," I reply confidently. There is no way he is turning me down tonight. His body language tells me he wants me as much as I want him.

I grind against his hard-on, kissing him deeper. His hands trail down my legs and shift under my skirt, cupping my bare ass, fingertips brushing against my lace G-string and pulling me down onto him.

"I love skirts," he mumbles in between kisses, and I break out in laughter. "I'm glad I can amuse you, even in the middle of sex." Maverick laughs, moving his kisses down the side of my throat.

I gasp, my laughter cutting off as he grinds his dick into me. "And I am not quite sure this is the middle of sex," I say, almost panting, breathless in reaction to his touch.

"No? Perhaps we should change that, then."

Maverick stands abruptly. I squeal and wrap my hands around his neck to hang on. His large hands cup my ass, and he supports my body as he starts walking.

"Where are we going?" I ask.

"To your bedroom, where you can be properly ravished," he says huskily.

"Mmm," I moan, licking a line up his neck.

As quickly as he picked me up, he drops me on my back onto what feels like my mattress, another squeal escaping as I fall out of his embrace. He is so caught up in this moment—so caught up with *me*—that he forgets to worry about manhandling me. He can manhandle me anytime. Clearly, I have some kinks that I cannot wait to explore with this man.

I lift my hands to the hem of my tank top, pushing it slowly up my abdomen, baring my skin to him slowly, hesitating when I get to my boobs. It's not like he hasn't seen them before, but does he even like them? Did he stop us from going further because he doesn't like the way I look?

"Keep going," he orders, his voice husky. I'm not going to disobey that voice.

I continue my path, revealing my bra to him and sitting up to remove it. I feel his arms wrap around me, quickly removing my bra and easing me back onto the bed. Maverick's touch is everywhere. His hands trail over my collarbone, followed by his mouth, and skim over my boobs, paying special attention to my puckered nipples. As he bites on one nipple, his hands drop and together we push off my skirt and panties.

His touches and kisses are gentle yet heated with desire. Maverick's body blankets mine, bringing his mouth back to mine, claiming my lips with a ferocious kiss. I feel deliciously scandalous with his fully clothed body pressed against my naked one. Being here with Maverick for my first time is everything I could wish for and more.

"Make love to me?" I whisper into his ear.

"Are you sure?" he asks.

"Yes," I moan, feeling only love and passion for him. "I have condoms in the top drawer."

Maverick stands, and I whimper at the lack of his weight on me. Being pinned down was unexpectedly exciting.

I lay there naked, listening to him undress, fish out a condom, and tear open the foil packet. Sitting up, I reach out to him.

"Can I help?" I ask hesitantly.

"Yes, here." He lines up the top of his cock and the condom, letting me roll the sleeve down the length of him. "Oh, baby. I love your hands on me," Maverick moans.

I grin up at him, tugging his dick a few times.

"Babe, you need to stop that if you want to have sex," Maverick says, gently pushing me back down to the bed and hovering over me again. A shiver racks my body at the feel of his cock against my inner thigh.

"Please," I whimper, feeling no shame at how much I need him. "Please, Maverick."

"What do you want, Cecilia?"

"I—I—" I pant, feeling my nipples brush against his chest hair and losing focus.

"Mm? You what, C?"

"I want you to consume me, to feel you in me, to fuck me and make me yours," I reply plainly, laying everything out for him.

"Let me know if I hurt you, okay?"

I nod wordlessly. His hand falls to my pussy, and he pushes his finger into me.

"Maverick," I complain, needing more. Needing all of him.

"I know, baby," He adds another finger, while his thumb brushes against my clit. I have never felt anything like this. His mouth claims mine, drinking in all my cries and moans. After a few minutes, he pulls his hand away and brings it to my lips.

"Taste yourself, baby."

I hesitate a second before cleaning his fingers with my tongue. He replaces his hand with his mouth, his tongue tangling with mine. The head of his cock nudging at my core, lighting me up inside.

I wrap my legs around his waist, drawing his body closer to mine—and finally, his cock inches into me. Softly, he pushes forward, leaving me breathless. I have never felt so much pain and pleasure at the same time.

"Are you okay?" he pants.

"Mmhmm," I reply, unable to utter any words.

Maverick keeps pushing until he is flush against my core and I hold all of him within me. He kisses me softly, teasing my tongue, our mouths growing more and more insistent as my body adjusts to his size.

"Can you move now?" I ask him, breaking the kiss.

"Yeah, babe." Maverick chuckles. "I just wanted to give you time."

"I'm good. Please."

I whimper at the loss as Maverick withdraws from my body. Before I have time to miss how full he makes me, he thrusts into me slowly, sensually, making love to me with his body. He manoeuvres our bodies to squeeze his hand between us, trailing his fingers over my clit. His calloused fingers create a friction I could never imagine. Heat flows through me, and unlike the first time he brought me to climax, my orgasm has no build-up, slamming into me as quickly as Maverick's thrusts.

I feel his lips curve into a smile against my neck, where he has been kissing, as I moan out his name.

"Oh, Maverick."

"Mmm, Cecilia."

"Whoa."

"I know, baby."

He lazily thrusts within me, keeping my body on a knife's edge, sensitive to his touch and ready to ignite again.

"I want you to ride me. Is that okay?" he asks, withdrawing from me.

I feel like I've lost a part of myself without him. "Will you teach me?" I ask.

"Yeah, baby." I can hear the smile in his voice.

He flops back onto the pillows and expertly lifts me up, positioning me above his still-erect cock.

"Can you grip my cock? Yes, like that. And angle it toward you more—you should be able to feel me brush against you." I follow his instructions, guiding the head of his cock back to my entrance, sighing as I line us up and begin to sink down on his dick.

"Oh, Cecilia," Maverick moans, his hands gripping my waist, my ass, my boobs, like he cannot get enough of me. And the feeling is mutual.

Maverick guides my hips, showing me how to rock against him —helping me position my legs to give me better leverage to pull myself up and down his throbbing cock. I lose myself in his touches, relishing his hands tracing my body. My palms are splayed across his chest, playing with his chest hair, feeling his muscles tense as he thrusts up into me.

"Fuck, fuck, fuck!" I chant as a tingling sensation starts in my toes and rushes through my whole body. I throw my head back and scream as Maverick brushes his thumb over my still-sensitive clit while his cock hits a spot inside me. My second orgasm overwhelms me, and Maverick takes over, holding my hips as he pumps up into me, a roar escaping him as we climax together. The feeling of his cock throbbing in me has me craving for us to be bare, to have his cum filling me, marking me, owning me.

I slump forward, covered in sweat, exhausted. My head falls against his chest and I can feel his heartbeat thrumming through him. He gently eases me off him and slowly gets out of bed. I hear him leave the room, and coldness washes over me.

"Open your legs for me, Cecilia," Maverick asks softly when he returns after a moment.

"Why?" I ask. He cannot be ready for a second round already —can he?

"I need to clean you up, baby," he explains. I allow my legs to fall open and feel him wipe me down with a warm washcloth. "You had a bit of blood, babe. Are you feeling okay?"

"I have never felt better," I tell him honestly, even with the slight ache in between my legs. Once he finishes, he throws the cloth in my laundry basket and lies down next to me in bed. Wrapping his arm around my shoulders, I use his chest as a pillow as I snuggle into his side. My body relaxes into him, our breaths evening out as Maverick places a final kiss on top of my head as I fall asleep in the arms of the man I love.

How could life ever get any better than this?

Seventeen - Maverick

I PLACE a kiss against Cecilia's fiery red hair. It looked even better than I imagined, fanned out on her pillows and framing our bodies as she rode me, curtaining us away from the rest of the world. My cock stirs at the memory. I ignore it as Cecilia's body sags against me, her breathing heavy as sleep claims her.

Just a few minutes, then I will wake her up and go home, I tell myself. I had wanted to tell her tonight—that was the reason I came inside. I wanted to sit with her on the couch and tell her who I am. Admittedly, I didn't try too hard to tell her before she seduced the pants off of me. My gorgeous, sexy, seductress little virgin. Well, not a virgin any longer.

Darkness tugs at the edges of my mind. I'll just rest a few minutes, then I'll go.

Buzz. Buzz. Buzz.

The sound of my phone ringing pulls me from a great dream of spending the night with my Cecilia. The ringing stops as my mind clears, and I realise I am wrapped around a warm, small body, my erection pressed against soft skin. I crack open my eyes to find myself in Cecilia's bed, spooning her as she stirs from her sleep. My phone starts ringing again, reminding me what woke me up in the first place.

I drag myself away from Cecilia's embrace, my eyes lingering on her sexy bare ass. The temptation to crawl back in bed with her is almost overwhelming if it wasn't for the insistent buzzing of my phone. I hadn't meant to stay the night, but I would be lying if I said I regretted it. I had forgotten how amazing it felt to be wrapped around someone I cared about all night.

I search the bedroom, rummaging through my discarded clothing to find my phone. My hand wraps around it just as it stops ringing.

Pulling it out of my pants, I tap the screen to see over thirty text messages from my brothers and two missed phone calls from Charlie. It's only 2 a.m., mere hours after Cecilia and I returned to her home. Panic surges through me. Ignoring the texts, I call Charlie straight back. He answers before it can finish one ring.

"Charlie, what's wrong? Is everyone okay?" I ask in an urgent whisper, quickly pulling on my briefs and stepping out of Cecilia's bedroom to not disturb her.

"We are all fine, Mav—it's you we are worried about. There was a photo posted of you tonight, out on your date with Cecilia."

"What?" My breath whooshes out of me. How could that be? I was so careful.

"Yeah bro, you were spotted. And it was posted online by a fan about an hour ago. Sites are already blowing up with your photo. They haven't identified Cecilia yet, but it won't take long for people who know her to put the pieces together."

"Fuck. Fuck. Fuck," I mutter. "I knew I should have told her already!"

"Maverick?" Cecilia says softly. I turn to see her standing in her doorway, a royal blue satin robe covering her.

"I gotta go, man. Thanks for letting me know," I say into the phone.

"Of course, Mav. Love you, bro."

"Love you too, Charlie." I hang up, glancing around the lounge room as if something there is going to be able to help me.

"Is everything okay?" Cecilia's soft voice settles the panic in me. I keep my eyes on her—hair messed and sex-crazed. *Not the time to get a boner, Maverick!*

"Yeah, babe, uh—we need to talk."

"What's wrong?"

"See, the thing is, there's something I need to tell you. I should have told you ages ago, but I was worried about how you would take it, and I kinda thought if I ignored it long enough, it would resolve itself."

"What is it?" Cecilia asks, dread clouding her face.

"I—"

"I KNEW IT." The front door bangs open and a young woman stands there, her appearance so similar to Cecilia that it has to be Taylor. She is wearing a black flowing blouse tucked into a burgundy pencil skirt that cuts off just beneath her knees. Her red hair is a few shades lighter than Cecilia's, with a more auburn undertone. Her eyes are jade green and are brimming with anger. It's 2 a.m.—she must have gone out after work, leaving me to wonder if she usually dresses like this or if she just didn't change after work.

"Taylor?" Cecilia asks. "What's happening? Why are you home so late?"

Taylor stalks towards me, her heels clicking against the tiles, slamming the door closed behind her and dropping her bag on the floor.

"You didn't!" Taylor's face drops, ignoring Cecilia's questions. I look down to realise I am only in my underwear, phone clutched in my hand so tightly it might break the screen.

"Don't!" I plead Taylor. "Please, I was about to—"

"Fat chance, you liar! Were you just taking advantage of her blindness like everyone else?"

"No, I swear! It's not like that."

"Taylor!? Maverick!? Will one of you please explain what the fuck is going on?"

"Maverick," Taylor scoffs. "At least you had the decency to tell her your real name. I can't believe it. Maverick... Watson."

"Watson," Cecilia whispers, her breath catching. "No. You can't be."

"I was about to tell you!"

"About to tell me that you aren't who I thought you were? Tell me that you are *the Mav* of Fly By! What the fuck was all this then? Some charity 'let's play house with the blind girl?'" Cecilia yells.

"No, I swear. It—"

"I don't want to hear it!"

"Please, C. It's not like that!" I plead.

"No?" she asks, voice dripping with sarcasm. "What is it like then, Maverick? Explain it to me, since I am so stupid!"

"I'm sorry, I never meant for it to go this far," I sob. Cecilia's face hardens, and I realise it was the wrong thing to say.

"You can go."

"C—"

"Cece—" Taylor says, concerned. We both talk at the same time, only to be cut off by Cecilia.

"NO!" Cecilia heads into her room, returning with a handful of my clothes and hers. "Take your clothes and leave, *Maverick*." My name dripping with loathing.

"But—" I protest, my eyes stinging with tears. This is what I feared would happen. Why didn't I tell her? Cecilia throws the clothes to the floor, returning to her room and closing the door behind her.

I fall to my knees on the floor, a sob wracking me. Tears fill my eyes and spill over, the words "I love you" on the tip of my tongue, but this isn't the time to say it. Cecilia won't believe me. She's already gone. Another girl who doesn't want me because of who I am.

Dejectedly, I gather my clothes from where they fell, feeling Taylor's eyes drilling holes into my back as I put them on.

"I care about her, Taylor. I swear I do. She is everything to me now."

Taylor scoffs. "Why should I believe you?"

It doesn't really matter if she believes me. "I feared the moment she knew it would ruin everything...guess I was right there. Usually, women only want the Mav they don't want *me*. Cecilia was—is—different. Fuck. I need to go."

I sidestep Taylor, leaving Cecilia's house for the last time, my heart in tatters and tears streaming down my cheeks as I get into my car and drive home. I lost the perfect girl for me, and there is no way I can fix it. I only have myself to blame.

Eighteen - Cecilia

"YOU KNOW you will have to talk to him eventually, Cecilia," Taylor says, interrupting my audiobook.

It has been a week since we had that overwhelming night. My first time was so special and perfect, only to be overshadowed. Maverick Watson. How could I have not figured it out?

"What am I going to say to him?" I reply. "I am hurt that he didn't feel like he could trust me, I am hurt that he was lying to me, and it has me overthinking what else he lied about. I feel like an idiot. Do you know how many times I went on and on to him about how amazing Fly By is? He probably was just with me as entertainment—something to laugh with his brothers about."

"You won't get any answers until you talk with him. I know I stormed in thinking he was taking advantage of you, but I don't know what to think, Cecilia. The look on his face when you threw him out…I've never seen anyone in more pain."

"I just don't know, Tay," I sigh, a flash of guilt filling me. The last thing I want to do was hurt Maverick—even after everything that happened. I should be glad he is gone. I shouldn't still be thinking about him. I should just move on and get over him.

"I can see how much you care about him," Taylor says. "Is it worth losing him over this? He respected your wishes and left that day. I think this time, it is up to you to reach out to him and get this settled. You won't be able to move forward—either in a relationship with him, or to get over him—without closure."

Crap, she is right, and she knows it. "Bitch," I mutter.

"Yes, but you love me anyway. Now I have to go to work. You are going to be okay by yourself, right?"

I can understand her concern. Apart from going to university, I have been a hermit for the last week, indulging in way too much ice cream and tormenting myself listening to romance novels that Maverick recommended to me—a mix of fantasy, historical, and contemporary stories. The asshole has good taste, and I can't help but think there was some hidden message in the books that he told me to read. Had he been trying to tell me something? I had been listening to the last one on his list when Taylor had come in to check on me.

"Yes, I will be fine tonight. Go."

"Okay, Cecilia. But remember to think about giving him a chance to explain. I know I barged in here overexcited and ruined your night, but I care about you, and I only want to see you happy again. I have never seen you as happy as you were when you were dating Maverick."

I flinch at her use of the past tense, but I sure am not seeing him now. After an amazing night of lovemaking, I threw him out on his ass.

"You need to ask yourself if you can forgive him," Taylor says, emphasizing her earlier question, "or if this lie is worth losing your relationship with him over." She kisses my forehead and leaves the room.

I sit there, overthinking again about all the time we spent together and how I didn't put the pieces together. All the money he spent, all the dates he organised. I realise now that we were always alone—except that last night together. There was never any other noise in a restaurant, no other people at the beach or park. That hadn't just been because we went at odd times or he knew a special spot, like I had thought. He had kept me out of the eye of the media.

Was he ashamed of me? Didn't want to be seen dating some blind nobody? *You know that's not true.* I did know. I know that I'm blowing this way out of proportion, but how can I just approach him now and act like I didn't fuck everything up?

Maverick's words come back to me. After what we had come to refer to as our first date, he stayed away from me for three weeks before coming back and saying, "I am not good enough for you. My life is a mess and there are things I need to tell you."

"And you told him he didn't need to tell you," I mutter to myself. I really am a fool.

Needing to get out of my head, I put my earphones back in and press play on the audiobook. It's a standalone novel about a partially deaf phone sex worker, who starts giving lessons in how to date to someone she met online. He had a very traumatic past and has zero confidence when speaking with women he's sexually attracted to.

No matter how much I focus on the book, my thoughts keep coming back to Maverick. Taylor is right. There is no way I am going to be able to do anything else until I talk with him. Taylor's parting words float in my mind. The question was never if I could forgive him—I already have. The question is could I trust him again...

I use my voice commands to pull up the contact list on my phone and hesitate. Is it too late or out of the blue to call him? Should I just wait until class on Wednesday? Maverick wasn't in class this week; the media's been abuzz, trying to figure out who his new girlfriend is—yet somehow, no one has figured out who I am yet. Will he even return to classes? If I wait, it'll be another three days of torturing myself with questions, and he might not even be there. I don't think I can wait that long.

Taking a deep breath, I call Maverick, holding the phone to my ear as it rings...and rings...and rings...

Nineteen - Maverick

I HAVE BEEN miserable all week. I sent Cecilia a text on Sunday asking her to give me a chance—a chance to explain, to apologise. She never replied, and since then, I've been keeping my distance. We still share classes together, and I still have to endure the sweet torture of being near Cecilia, but not with her.

My week was hectic, Mitch and our PR team helped with the media, releasing some information out about the tour to distract the world from trying to identify Cecilia. I had to skip university to keep the paparazzi who were following me away from her, and—I am only slightly ashamed to admit—to avoid Cecilia. I don't think I could handle being so close to her and seeing her ignore me. Or worse, what if she's just indifferent?

I would give anything to hear her say my name again in that soft way of hers, to hold her hand or brush my fingertips through her hair. I have gone over that night in my head so many times. I should have told her who I was before we had sex, I should have told her who I was weeks ago, when I knew I was falling for my sweet Cecilia. Now, I have lost what was becoming the most important thing to me.

I wish she gave me the chance to explain everything to her that night, but what would I have said in the heat of the moment? "I thought you would turn into a stalker?" That was true at first, but once I got to know her—I knew that wasn't who she is. My only hope now is waiting for Cecilia to reach out to me and give me time to tell her the truth. Not that I deserve it, but how can I just give up on her? How can I just move on like she meant nothing?

I missed out on family lunch last Sunday, as I had been too distraught over everything happening with Cecilia, but today my brothers literally forced me. They showed up at my apartment, pushed me into the shower to get ready, and are now driving my ass up to Mum and Dad's place.

I am suffocating under the pressure of their concern and empathy. I don't deserve their pity. I did this to myself. I deserve to be upset over the pain I caused C.

I pulled up Cecilia's contact in my phone, reading through our message thread like I don't already have it memorised. Tom reaches over and snatches my phone out of my hands.

"Hey! I'm not going to do anything!" I protest.

"I saw that look in your eyes—you were going to message her. How many times have you been about to message her this week?" Tom asks, and I remain silent. "That's what I thought," Tom replies, turning back in his seat and placing my phone in his pocket. "You can get this back later today. Get your mind off her today. Tormenting yourself isn't going to change anything."

I slump in my seat and stare out the window. Am I acting like a child? Yes. Do I care? Not one bit. Thankfully, the boys remain silent. Tom really is the best person to hold onto my phone for me; he has more self-control than I do. Even at eighteen, he is the most rational one out of the five of us, always ready to tell you what you need to hear—especially if it's not something you want to hear.

I am on edge. I just want to go into the garage and play out my emotions—or to try, anyway. I barely had the motivation to write or play all week, hiding out in my apartment, which is strange for me. Normally, writing lyrics is the best way to process my emotions, so I write no matter what I feel. I am not sure if I want to move on from these emotions. I sure as hell don't want to move on from Cecilia.

The second I step in the front door, Mum's arms wrap around me and I sag into her, drawing the comfort I have denied myself all week.

"Hi, baby," she coos in my ear. "How are you doing?"

"I'm fine."

"He is not fine. His apartment is a pigsty, and I'm sure he hasn't showered in days. It's all because *she* won't speak to him," Charlie tells Mum.

I whip around to face him. "Do *not* speak of Cecilia in that tone!" I seethe.

Charlie grins, clearly glad to have gotten a reaction out of me.

"He is touchy today, Mum," Joel helpfully adds.

"Shut up!" I growl. Fed up with my brothers, I brush past my family and retreat into the garage.

I pick up my Gibson by the neck as I move around the room, turning amps on and picking up a pick from the stack on the table. I play haphazardly, aggressively striking chord after chord, not caring how loud they are or what sound they make. After a while, my fingers start picking out new chords, forming a new melody…a new song born of my love. My pain. My Cecilia.

When I am mentally worn out and can't play any longer, I reluctantly leave the garage and join my family, knowing I can't avoid them forever. Only a few hours have passed, but I am surprised that my brothers left me alone in the garage for that long. Clearly, they don't want to be around me right now any more than Cecilia does.

I follow their voices and walk in to find them sitting around the dining room table, Mum just laying the last dish on to the table.

"I was just about to come and get you," Mum says, turning to me. "Lunch is ready, sweetie." She hesitates, and I can see her desire to hug me and take away the pain. She has always been the best mum.

"Thanks, Mum," I say, placing a kiss against her cheek before sitting down in my usual seat. Silence falls as we do our usual routine of filling our plates with food, today's spread a roast lamb shoulder and a variety of roast and steamed vegetables.

"So, are you going to tell us what happened or what?" Ethan asks, breaking the tense silence.

"Ethan!" Mum scolds him.

"What? It's not like we aren't all wondering," Ethan replies, glaring at me. "It has been radio silence from him. You have always said talking about something helps, Mum. So tell us, Mav."

"E—"

"No, Mum, it's okay," I cut her off. "Better to get it out in the open now, I guess." I pause, taking a moment to think everything over. "I was on the phone with Charlie when Cecilia came out of the bedroom, concerned about what was going on. I was about to tell her when her sister, Taylor, busted into the house. She saw the photos and told Cecilia before I could.

C flipped her shit. I deserved it. I had been planning on telling her for weeks, but I just couldn't think of a way to bring it up without losing her. And I lost her anyway..." I trail off, taking in the faces of my family around me. None of them are angry with me, but they don't pity me as much anymore either.

"I don't know what to tell you, son," Dad says from his seat at the head of the table. "I imagine—" Dad is cut off by the shrill ringing of Tom's phone.

"Tom, you know there's no phones during family meals!" Mum tells him as he pulls out the phone. Tom's eyes bulge out as he looks at the screen, flicking up to look at me and around the room, then dropping back to the phone in his hands.

"I—I need to take this. Sorry, Mum," Tom replies, standing so quickly he tips over his seat before rushing out of the room.

Glad to have the attention off me for now, I shovel mash potatoes into my mouth. I wish I came here earlier in the week now—nothing fixes anything like Mum's cooking. Plus, I feel better having my family aware of my situation. I shouldn't have hidden anything from Cecilia or my family. It's true what they say—hindsight really is a bitch.

Twenty - Cecilia

RING...RING...RING...

I am about to give up when he finally picks up. I can hear his heavy breathing, but he doesn't say anything.

"Maverick?" I ask tentatively. "Are you there?"

A grunt is the only response I receive, and really, what else can I expect. He probably thinks I am calling to yell at him again. I never gave him the chance to explain on Sunday, after all, ignoring his text and presence at uni all week.

"Look, Maverick, I was hoping we could meet up and chat about everything? I am sorry I never gave you the chance to explain the other day. But—"

"What are you going to say to him?" a gruff voice asks. A voice that isn't Maverick.

"Wh-who's this?"

"Tom—Tom Watson, Maverick's brother."

"Why are you answering his phone? Is he okay?"

"I took it off him to prevent him from calling you. He has not been himself all week, and before I tell him you called, I need to know what you plan on doing. Are you going to give him a second chance? Let him explain to you why he concealed his identity? Are you only crawling back to him because of who he is and his money and fame? Maverick has always been our protector, and this time I am going to protect him, even if that means he needs to be protected from you."

I sob into the phone, "I'm sorry! I need to talk with him, to fix this. But"—I hiccup— "I need to understand first."

"Okay, shh. I didn't mean to make you cry! Fuck. Mav will kill me if he knows I upset you," Tom says, his words rushing out.

"I'm sorry," I mutter, reining in my tears. "I was going to ask him to meet me so we can talk. Can he come here? Or I can come to him? I need to talk to him. Please," I almost beg.

"We are up at Orlo at our parents' house at the moment, so he won't be back in the city until tonight."

"That's okay! Anytime—as soon as he can get here. Anything. Please?"

"Hmm…" Tom pauses for a moment. "We drove him up here, I think I can work something out. What's your address?"

I give him my address and hope that this is the right decision.

"I hope you know what you are doing," Tom says, hanging up the phone before I can respond.

"Me too," I mutter into the silence. "Me too."

I spend the next few hours getting ready for Maverick to come over. I shower and put on new clothes, straighten up my bed and make sure all my dirty clothes are in the laundry basket. I putter around, keeping my hands busy. I sweep, I mop—not that I can really tell if the floor is clean. After three hours, I sit back down on the couch, turning on a mindless talk show that doesn't require me to pay much attention but fills the silence in the house. I'm out of options except to sit and wait for him now.

It feels like an eternity has passed when I hear yelling outside. Unable to make out the voices, I turn off the TV and open the door to hear a jumble of men yelling. I am about to close the door when I make out one voice—*the* voice.

Maverick is here.

"Why the fuck did you bring me here?" Maverick seethes, I can feel the fury and pain radiating off him. "How do you even know her address?"

"You need to speak with her, man," Tom replies. I recognise his voice from the phone and put it together: he brought Maverick here.

"That's not your call to make! You four assholes know she doesn't want to speak with me."

"That's not true," I interject, feeling five sets of eyes turn to me.

One of his brother's wolf-whistles, stopping abruptly as I hear a punch and an "oof" escapes them.

"Cecilia…" Maverick speaks, saying my name like a prayer.

"I called you earlier," I explain. "Tom answered, and I asked him to help give me the opportunity to talk to you."

"Why didn't you tell me, dickhead?" Maverick growls.

"Because I didn't know if you would go through with it!" Tom replies snarkily. "You know, like you went through with actually telling her about being in Fly By?"

They start yelling again. This is clearly not going to go anywhere. How did their parents survive raising them all in one household?

"CHARLIE, JOEL, TOM, ETHAN!" I call out to get their attention. "It's nice to meet you all, but I need you all to kindly fuck off right now so I can speak with my man."

"She's perfect for you," someone whispers.

"Thank you." I almost preen. "Maverick?"

"Your man?" he asks, surprised.

"Yes, Maverick. Inside, please. You boys can leave. He can find another way home."

"Thanks, bro. I'm sorry." I hear a few back slaps and footsteps fading away until it's just me standing in my open doorway, and Maverick standing a few steps away.

Turning, I walk into the house, knowing he will follow, and find my way to the couch. The couch dips under his weight as he shifts in his seat. All my thoughts—all my preparation—just evaporates from my mind. I wring my fingers anxiously. Now that he is finally here, I have no idea what I want to say.

"Cecilia?" Maverick's warm voice washes over me, settling my nerves and replacing them with anticipation.

"Hi Maverick," I say nervously.

"How have you been?"

"Pretty wretched." I laugh self-deprecatingly. His hands clasp mine and cease my twitching, his rough fingers stroking my soft skin. "You?"

"I have been miserable, and before you yell at me again, I need you to know I am sorry. You weren't meant to find out that way. Not telling you earlier is the biggest regret of my life.

I was so worried about everything else that was happening that I lost the best thing to ever happen to me."

"What's the best thing to happen to you?" Did they lose their label deal? I have only seen tabloids about me and the upcoming tour this week.

"You, you goose." Maverick chuckles affectionately, running the pad of his thumb over my wrist.

"M-me?" I stammer.

"My last week without you has been utter hell, baby. I don't know why you needed to speak with me, but you need to know I am so sorry."

Taking a deep breath, I ask, "Why did you do it?"

"I wish I had a good answer for you." Maverick sighs, the couch moving as he twists around. "When we first met, I knew there was something special about you. I felt like myself for the first time in years. I'm not going to lie—for a moment there, I thought you might only want me because I was in Fly By, or use me for connections in the music industry, like others have. I pulled back, thinking it was better for both of us to not be involved. I didn't want you to have to deal with the paparazzi bombarding your life or tabloids writing about you. And I didn't want to get hurt again. That first day showed me that you had the ability to twist me in knots. All my life, I have been looking for my own real-life romance story, and—"

"And meeting me wasn't that for you," I finish for him, hurt. It had been that and so much more for me.

"That's not it, C," Maverick rushes to reassure me. One of his hands lifts and cups my face. "You *are* it for me. I was half in love with you after our first day together. I couldn't keep myself away from you, no matter what lies I told myself. I still had to be near you and know you were okay. I never planned to lie to you for so long. I thought if I kept it from you for a little bit, you would get to know the real me, not held up on my status or fame. I enjoyed being normal with you—dating like a regular couple, getting to know what an amazing person you are, falling in love with you more and more every day."

"You hurt me, Maverick," I say softly.

"I know, Cecilia, and I will never stop being sorry for that. I thought that you—"

"That I would be a vapid, shallow bitch who only stuck around for your fame and money?" I ask, my anger slowly rising again.

"I—uh—I know you wouldn't, but I doubted myself, not you. I couldn't figure out why someone like you would want to be with someone like me."

"Someone like me?" I yell. "What's that supposed to mean, Maverick? Someone so beneath you? Someone poor?" I push his hands off me, getting to my feet.

"No! Please! That's not what I meant, C. Please, baby." His voice hitches as he stands from the couch. "P-please, baby. That's not it. I love you, Cecilia." He cups my face again. I wrap my hands around his wrists to pull him away, ignoring his declaration. This has gone too far. I drop his hands and step back from him.

"I asked you to come here so I could apologise for not giving you the chance to explain and see if we could work this out. But—"

"Cecilia," Maverick says firmly, "I meant that I didn't know why someone as perfect, as beautiful, as unique, as charming, as astonishing as you would want to be with someone like me, who would just turn your life upside-down and has the reputation of a womaniser. I didn't mean to hurt you or make you think I have been playing games with you. From the beginning, I have been all in with you. I meant to tell you, and I am sorry it came out the way it did, but I am glad you know now. Do you think you could ever forgive me?"

Could I? I find myself in the place I was in this morning. Yes, I've already forgiven him, but I don't know if I would be able to trust him. Would he keep things from me again? Tentatively, I reach out and place my hands on his face, a shudder running up my spine. His cheeks are wet with his tears, pooling in his beard and giving it a different texture. This is Maverick: both sides of him, together. My Maverick and the one from Fly By.

I could pull back, never hear from him again, and be miserable with my life. Or I could leap, put faith in him, and be with the man I love.

"Never lie to me again," I murmur. I twist my hands into his hair.

"I won't. I promise."

"I forgive you, Maverick."

"You do?"

"Yes. And—"

"And? And?"

"I love you too," I say, finally acknowledging his earlier words. I pull his face toward mine, crashing my lips against his. Being within his arms—where I belong—has never felt so right.

Twenty-One - Maverick

HOW DID I survive twenty-two years without her touch, but after a week I feel like a starving man? I fall into her kiss, her touch. I feel like I am coming home after a long tour.

Her hands pull at my hair, the jolt of pain shooting straight to my cock. I reluctantly break the kiss. "Where's Taylor?"

"She's out for work or something. She won't be back until later. Do you want to go to my room?"

I will never deny this girl something she wants ever again. "Okay, baby."

She pulls away from me and saunters to her bedroom, and I trail behind her, watching her ass sway. Before I have the door closed, Cecilia pulls off her T-shirt, showcasing her electric-blue bra to me.

"W-what are we doing, C?" I ask, not sure what she wants to do and not wanting to push her now that I finally have her back. I pinch myself just to check if this is a dream or not.

Nope. Not dreaming. Cecilia is standing in front of me in denim shorts and a bra. Talk about what dreams are made of.

"I need you, Maverick. Even with everything that happened, it's been on my mind all week. I need to feel you on me—in me. Please?" she begs, and what was left of my self-control vanishes.

I cross the room, palming her beautiful tits with both hands as I crush my mouth to hers. I claim her mouth, invading her with my tongue, tasting her sweetness. I pinch her nipples through her bra, causing her to moan into my mouth. Her hands grip at my shirt, yanking the fabric up.

"Off," Cecilia mutters into my mouth.

I laugh lightly as I pull back, removing my shirt. When I return my hands to her chest, I meet skin, and I realise she took the opportunity to remove her bra.

Naked from the hips up, we embrace each other again. I palm her breasts, rolling her peaked nipples through my fingers, groaning as I feel her soft hands trail over my stomach.

"Please," she whimpers.

"Please what?" I tease.

"Ugh!" Cecilia groans in protest, her hands dropping to my waistband. Slipping inside, she manages to undo my button and fly before I can even respond.

She hooks her thumbs in and pulls down my jeans and briefs at once, not bothering to get them past mid-thigh before her small fist wraps around my aching cock.

"Please put this in me!" she demands, tugging on my cock, running her thumb over the dribble of precum leaking out.

I moan as I undo her shorts, noticing she is bare underneath.

"No panties?" I ask, dipping my fingers into her slit.

"Uh-uh," she replies breathlessly.

"Naughty girl," I growl, picking her up by the waist and throwing her onto the bed. Her loose hair spreads across the doona, her naked body beckoning me to ravish her. To bury my cock so deep in her, she will never forget me. To claim and own her body.

I stand for a moment, tracing her body with my eyes, just admiring her every curve, every freckle.

"Mine."

"Are you going to come and take what is yours?" Cecilia asks innocently.

Without any hesitation, I fall on top of her, plastering every inch of our naked bodies together, our mouths joining again. My cock rubs against her thigh, drawing a moan from me.

Reaching for the bedside table, I pull out a condom quickly, tearing the packet open and putting it on. There is no way I would last if Cecilia put it on me this time.

Cecilia squeals as I grab her waist and flip her over to her stomach. I didn't take her from behind last time, and right now I think we both need it hard and fast. I ease my finger into her, feeling her tight, wet heat.

"More!" she complains.

"I don't want to hurt you, baby." Her body still needs more time to get used to my cock.

"Please, Maverick, I need you."

Giving in, I line up my cock with her entrance, slowly easing in as I trail kisses over her shoulder blades and the back of her neck. I push forward gently as she exhales, inch by inch. I pause when there is nothing more to give her.

"Oh, just fuck me already, please!" Cecilia begs, causing me to chuckle.

"I have created a monster," I murmur into her ear, nibbling on her earlobe.

"Please. I don't care if it hurts. I just need you to move, to fuck me, to feel you claim me."

It's like she's speaking from my dirtiest fantasies.

"I was actually giving *me* a moment, but—" I break off as I pull out and slam roughly into her.

Cecilia calls out, screaming in pleasure as I thrust into her again and again. My hands trail up and down her spine, squeezing her ass as I thrust into her. Tantalising sounds fill the room, encouraging me and increasing my pleasure. I hear my balls slapping against her clit, joining the sounds of her wet pussy swallowing my dick and our combined groans of pleasure.

"Ma-a-a-v," Cecilia whimpers. Her walls clench around me, tightening her even more.

Pulling out, I flip her back onto her back. Sitting back on my knees, I wrap my hand under her body, trailing my middle finger across her clit as I re-enter her tight heat.

"Mav, I-I-I'm—" Cecilia pants.

"Cum for me, baby," I groan. "Cum on my dick." With two more swipes over her clit, her orgasm wracks her body. Hovering over her, I place my arms on either side of her head. I kiss her, claiming her mouth and tongue with mine. Her body vibrates as she moans into my mouth, her pussy clenching me so tight it is almost painful as she draws my orgasm out of me, milking my cock. I slam into her again, drawing out our pleasure as long as possible.

I gingerly pull out of her, and we both sag onto the mattress, gravitating toward each other. I tie off the condom, dropping it to the floor before she curls up in the crook of my arm, her head on my chest.

"I love you, Maverick Watson of Fly By. For the man you are inside, for all of you: the romantic and the musician," Cecilia murmurs sleepily, soothing all my nerves and fears at once.

"I love you, Cecilia." I drift off to sleep in my Cecilia's arms.

Twenty-Two - Cecilia

"ARE YOU SURE THIS IS OKAY?" I ask Maverick, rubbing my sweaty palms against my jeans.

"Yes, baby, they all want to meet you." He places his hand over mine, stilling my fidgeting. We are on our way to his childhood home for their weekly Sunday lunch—which now includes me, apparently. It has been a week since Maverick and I made up, and this week has been a whirlwind. "Besides, you technically already met my brothers."

"I yelled at them, though. They must hate me."

"They don't hate you. They are happy for us—trust me."

"I can't believe I am meeting Fly By," I say, almost vibrating in my seat, full of nerves.

"Oh, I get it, you are excited to meet *them*. How come you didn't get starstruck over me?"

"Well, you are just Maverick to me. Not this all-powerful rock star," I tease. Truthfully, it has been a challenge to adapt my Maverick to being the Mav of Fly By. I spend ages replaying our dates and conversations, trying to comprehend how I landed this famous guitarist.

"You ready?" Maverick asks as the car pulls to a stop.

"As ready as I will ever be," I mutter, taking a deep breath and getting out of the car. I extend my cane as I wait for Maverick to meet me at the passenger door. I wrap my hand around his elbow, falling into the comfortable groove we have now. The familiarity of Maverick's skin on mine and his spoken directions about bumps and steps as we walk up his parents' driveway soothes me. I am safe here with him.

I hear loud voices through the house as Maverick opens the front door, leading me into the house.

All conversation stops suddenly, and I can feel everyone's eyes on us. I want to shrink into Maverick's side. How did he think this was a good idea?

"Well, now I understand," a young male voice says, and I tense, waiting for the onslaught.

"Understand what, Ethan?" Maverick asks, putting a name to the voice for me.

"Why you lied for so long. Wowzah. I thought you looked good on your porch, Cecilia, but dayum, girl. What are you doing with a loser like Maverick?" Ethan replies.

"Uh—I don't know what to say to that," I reply honestly. "I thought you were going to point out that I am blind."

"Well, that's just a part of the beautiful package that you are," another voice says.

"Dude," Maverick interjects. I hear him shift forward, and then a slap. "Stop hitting on my girlfriend."

Girlfriend. I almost sigh. I don't think I will ever get tired of hearing that.

"Ooooooh, does big bad Maverick have a giiiirrrlfrriiieeend?" a new voice calls out, exaggerating the word.

"Yes, Charlie. Don't be a dick just because you are jealous," Maverick says, claiming my hand in his larger one.

"He's not jealous," Tom starts, and I identify his voice from our previous conversations. "We all know he has his eyes on a certain someone—"

"Maverick, baby!" a woman coos, cutting Tom off.

"Hi Mum," Maverick replies softly, letting me go to embrace his mother. "This is Cecilia," he introduces. "Cecilia, this is my mum, Odette."

"Hi sweetie," she says to me. "Well, aren't you just gorgeous. Can I hug you?"

"I, uh—yeah?" I reply, handing Maverick my cane and awkwardly holding out my arms. Soft, small arms wrap around me, smelling of citrus and roses, and I sense a woman roughly the same height as me.

"Welcome to our home. Thank you for taking a chance on our Maverick," she whispers into my ear before pulling back and releasing me.

"And this is my dad, Griffin," Maverick says.

"Please call me Griff, or Dad. Hardly anyone calls me Griffin these days," a gruff voice replies. I extend my free hand and receive a soft handshake. "It's a pleasure to meet you, Cecilia."

"Th-thank you," I reply, feeling at ease and overwhelmed all at once.

"And you kinda already know the others: Tom, Ethan, Joel, and Charlie." They all come up and shake my hand, saying hello or introducing themselves so I can familiarise myself with their voices.

Lunch goes on without a hitch, Maverick taking the time to tell me what is available on the table and filling my plate up with loads of delicious food. Conversation floats between the family, continuously asking me questions and including me.

"Do you want to come into the garage and listen to band prac?" Maverick practically purrs in my ear once lunch is over.

"If you are sure that's okay?" I ask, barely containing my excitement. This is a private show and front-row seat to my favourite band!

"Of course, baby!"

Maverick leads me into the garage, pulling up a seat for me in the "perfect spot," as he says. Once the brothers are all ready, they murmur among themselves before breaking into my favourite song, "Seen." The words mean more to me now, knowing that Maverick wrote them.

"I built walls so high I couldn't see the sky, tore apart my heart so it wouldn't break.

I can talk the talk and walk the walk, but I've never felt at home in my own skin.

ALL I WANT IS someone to show me all I am, to show what I could be, so I can...

. . .

SEE ME! Help me! Step forward into the light tell me everything's alright.

Then one day, the world will! See me!

And accept all that I've become before I come undone, so please let me."

They play for hours, running through songs I have heard before and new ones that must be going on their new album. Odette enters the garage halfway through, bringing me a bottle of water.

Maverick wraps his arms around me once they finish their set list, his sweat accentuating the scent of citrus and leather that is purely him.

"So how was that?" he asks me, placing a soft kiss against my lips.

"I have never had a more perfect day," I answer truthfully, not caring if his brothers overhear me.

"Here, have this," Maverick says, placing his guitar pick in my hand. I practically vibrate with joy. A memento for me to keep. I don't think I will ever get over the fact that my boyfriend is in Fly By. "Do you remember what I asked you the day we met?" he asks gruffly.

"Uh, you asked me a lot of questions that day, Maverick. Help me out here?" I giggle.

"I asked you who your favourite Fly By member was after I told you I knew them."

"Yes, you did. Your point?"

"Is Joel still your favourite?" Maverick asks hesitantly.

"No," I say, deadpan. "No, definitely not. It's Tom now."

"What?" His voice is strained.

I burst out laughing, unable to hold myself together any longer. "You are my favourite, Maverick." I stretch up to kiss his cheek, but Maverick meets my mouth with a kiss instead.

Epilogue - Cecilia

"LADIES AND GENTLEMEN, I present to you: The Class of 2020!" the dean announces, completing our graduation ceremony. I squeal in excitement with my fellow graduates and wait for my family to find me in the crowd.

"You did it, baby girl!" my father cheers as he greets me with a hug.

"I am so proud of you, Cecilia!" my Mum adds, hugging me too.

As she releases me, and before Taylor can say hello, strong arms wrap around me, picking me up and spinning me around as I laugh. Maverick's scent wafts over me with his embrace. I faintly hear my parents' protests.

"Congratulations, C!" Maverick says, putting my feet back on the ground.

"Hi!" I laugh, turning back towards my parents. "Mum, Dad, this is Maverick, my boyfriend. Mav, this is Sally and Phillip."

"It's nice to meet you both," Maverick says, greeting them briefly before turning back to me. "I am heading out for dinner with my family. Did you all want to join?"

"That sounds great," I reply, gladly accepting for all of us.

"Great!" Maverick says, placing an all-too-innocent-for-my-liking kiss against my lips and rushing off to find his family.

We enter the Spanish restaurant to find that Maverick has privately hired the whole restaurant for the night, giving the brothers the freedom to relax and enjoy celebrating without worrying about wandering cameras or interrupting fans.

My parents were shocked when I told them about dating Maverick. At first they were concerned about his fame, which I can understand. But Taylor helped me set them straight, telling them that this is something that I can handle.

After introductions are made, my parents sit with Odette and Griff while Taylor sits between me and Charlie. The restaurant has a set menu for us tonight, and conversation flows around the table as waiters bring out a variety of tapas to start.

"Now, a little bit of nepotism at work," Maverick addresses me after the first course, "but I hope you don't mind—I organised an interview for you with Reckless Tunez. They are looking for a new agent. I insisted that even though you are my girlfriend, they interview you like all the other candidates. You just have to show them your amazing self and I think they will love you. Besides, I thought that with you working for them we may be able to get you to come on tour with us…" he trails off, no doubt taking in my shocked expression.

"You want me to come on tour with you?" I ask breathlessly.

"Of course I do, babe," he rambles nervously. "I would happily just support you financially, but I know working in the industry is something that you want to do. Is that okay? If you don't want to work with the same label, I get that too. I can help you apply somewhere else."

"Of course I want to go on tour and work with you!" I exclaim.

Maverick kisses me with a passion that takes my breath away, no longer caring that both of our families are here. Catcalls come out of his brothers, only encouraging Maverick. How did this become my life? I know one thing for certain: Maverick running into me was the best thing that could have ever happened to me.

The End.

Interested in what happens next with the Fly By Boys?

Stay tuned.
Joel is up next with "Hear Me"!

Seen

I'm in a cold dark room surrounded by people I've never met. Encompassed yet so alone. Hidden behind a mask my smile shines through to appear that I'm alright.

All I want is someone's eyes to dissolve all I am, take me apart piece by piece, put back all my fragments and...

See me! Help me! Step forward into the light tell me everythings alright. Then one day, the world will! See me! And accept all that Ive become before I come undone, so please just.

I build walls so high I couldn't see the sky, tore apart my heart so it wouldn't break. I can talk the talk and walk the walk but I've never felt at home in my own skin.

All I want is someone to show me all I am, to show what I could be, so I can...

See me! Help me! Step forward into the light tell me everythings alright. Then one day, the world will! See me! And accept all that Ive become before I come undone, so please let me.

Don't wait on me I'll never make it over. To self obsessed with how get over - all these years of hiding all that I am. I wanna break out and shout to the heavens!

I see me! I'll help me! Step forward into the light tell me everythings alright. Todays the one day, the world will! See me! And accept all that Ive become I'll never run away from me.....

Inverted

"Damn guys get a load this of this one, hey there sugar!"
I'm the type of guy that can bring you to you knees. Begging
"please please please!"
I'm not your lord or saviour but I'm hearing your prayers.
Tonight's all I care about is getting you out of that dress ...but
leave on those boots.

I'd love see the inside of you, would you like me too?

Did you wanna be, did you wanna be my baby?
Cause I wanna be, I wanna be your daddy!
I'm burning hot, gimme whatchu got and I'll lay it on real
smooth.
Ill take you down, I'll make you move, and I'll spin you round.
Inverted!

I've never seen a woman move the way that you do.
With your body so sweet that I'd never forget the taste too.
The things you do to my head, when your in my bed.

Inverted

Some would think that your sucking up for something......Oh
wait ...

Did you wanna be, did you wanna be my baby?
Cause I wanna be, I wanna be your daddy!
I'm burning hot, gimme whatchu got and I'll lay it on real
smooth.
Ill take you down, I'll make you move, and ill spin you round.
Inverted!

I thought I'd be the one using you, but it seems that we've
swapped
Making you my lil toy that I'd wind up and watch.
You've got a devilish tongue, that you've wrapped around me
and man "I hate it when she does that"
And now I'm so damn deep that I'll never leave.
So...

Cause your gonna be, your gonna be my baby.
And I wanna be, I wanna be your daddy!
I'm burning hot, gimme whatchu got and I'll lay it on real
smooth.
Ill take you down, I'll make you move, and I'll spin you round.
Inverted!
Oh ... We're Inverted!

Runaway

Brown heels, curly hair, eyes so blue you'd think they're the ocean.
I found you in a cafe downtown, my heartbeat stopped, and the world lost its sound.
Fell in love at first sight, don't know who you are but that's alright.
Are you even a fan of people like me? Long hair, dark clothes and all inked from my head to my feet...
Will you....

Runaway tonight! Let's runaway tonight
Runaway tonight! Let's runaway tonight

I know people might not like the way that you walk, the way that you dress,
but you're a best thing I've ever seen baby.
We'll be followed by paparazzi and cheap magazines, you don't gotta worry cause I'll show you the real me. So when they're following us we'll just...

Runaway tonight! Let's runaway tonight.

Runaway tonight! Let's runaway tonight
And if they ever come knocking on our front door I'll go give
em what's for and make them ...
Runaway tonight! Go on runaway tonight.

We'll be Bonnie and Clyde, ride till we die. Make sweet love
every night.
Talk about life and the weight of it all. Drive with the top
down or fly to Nepal.
As long as we got each other, one way or another. There ain't
nothing in this life that's gonna bring us down. So let's just...

Runaway tonight! Let's runaway tonight
Runaway tonight! Let's runaway tonight
And I'll be ok, even though I watched you runaway from me,
I'll be here waiting for you so we can...
Runaway tonight! Let's runaway tonight
Runaway tonight! Let's runaway tonight

Acknowledgments

WOW! Another book accomplished, and it has been a
whirlwind.
The last six months of 2020 were absolute crap for me, and
for a while I wasn't sure if I would get this book finished for
my self-imposed deadline—but here we are!
A huge thanks to my big brother Lukasz Muller who wrote the
Fly By songs for me—you helped me bring my Fly By Boy's to
life and honestly you are amazing at what you can do with an
instrument. Love you always no matter how dorky you are.
Thank you to each and every one of my readers! You have
helped me realise a lifelong passion and I wouldn't be here
without you.
As always, a very huge thank you to my partner in all things,
my Hayden. You are my own real life romance novel, I am so
blessed that I found you and get to keep you in my life.
To my beautiful betas, Isabou and Bec thank you for being my
own personal hype squad. You never fail to cheer me on and
give me the encouragement to continue. Thank you for always
taking the time to read my words and support me on my
journey!
Thanks also to Bee, from BlindBeta on Tumblr who helped

ensure this book portrayed vision impairment accurately, without bias or stereotypes.

To the endless list of friends and family—thank you for your support, encouragement and challenging me when I needed it. Especially my parents and in-laws, Adele, Cathie and Jeff, Martin and Treena, I would not be the person I am without you all.

About the Author

Heidi grew up in south-west Sydney, Australia, and now lives in the Southern Highlands of NSW with her marvellous boyfriend, Hayden. Heidi is a dog mum to two beautiful, attention loving girls, Amber and Daisy. Unfortunately, Amber passed away while in the editing stage of this book. Heidi is 24 and has 2 brothers and a sister.
Heidi had difficulties learning and maintaining the standard literacy and numeracy requirements in school, until she found her love for reading. It all started with a cringe worthy obsession over a certain Edward Cullen, which has fuelled Heidi to go on to reading 200+ books a year.
With a passion for reading, Heidi began writing short stories, and has always had an overactive imagination. Heidi comes across as a loud, boisterous person, who is actually a shy girl terrified of rejection. This fear held Heidi captive for a long time and prevented Heidi from sharing any of her work - until 2020.
With two previous books published, and a new series on the way, Heidi cannot wait to share the inner desires of her mind with you all.

Follow Me!

Want to keep up with all the new releases from H. L. Muller? Make sure you sign up for her newsletter for all the latest on upcoming books:
www.hlmullerauthor.com
Or you can check out her social media:
www.instragram.com/heidilmuller
www.facebook.com/hlmuller.author
www.goodreads.com/author/show/20148777.H_L_Muller